Darcy sighed  **stay here.'**

'So do you.'

Silence.

Then, suddenly, a germ of an idea was whirring in the back of Susie's mind. 'There is one other way,' she said slowly.

'One other way of what?'

'Of getting you immigration status. Of you being permitted to work here. Of all of us being able to work here together.'

He stared at her in the moonlight. She looked almost ethereal—a fairy at the bottom of the garden. A very pregnant fairy wearing spotted pyjamas... Despite himself, Darcy couldn't suppress a grin and she saw it.

'There's no need to laugh,' she retorted. 'This is a very serious proposition, and it could just work.'

'How could it work?' Darcy enquired.

'You could marry me.'

Marion Lennox has had a variety of careers—medical receptionist, computer programmer and teacher. Married, with two young children, she now lives in rural Victoria, Australia. Her wish for an occupation which would allow her to remain at home with her children, her dogs, the cat and the budgie led her to attempt writing a novel. Marion also writes under the same name for Mills & Boon® Tender Romance™.

Recent titles by the same author:

DOCTOR ON LOAN

EMERGENCY WEDDING

BY
MARION LENNOX

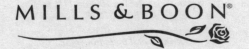

MILLS & BOON®

First published in Great Britain 2001
Harlequin Mills & Boon Limited,
Eton House, 18-24 Paradise Road, Richmond, Surrey TW9 1SR

© Marion Lennox 2001

ISBN 0 263 82697 X

Set in Times Roman 10¼ on 11¼ pt.
03-1101-51854

Printed and bound in Spain
by Litografia Rosés, S.A., Barcelona

CHAPTER ONE

WELCOME home banners? Confetti showers? Yellow ribbons tied to old oak trees?

Whale Beach had prepared none of the traditional welcome home displays for Dr Susie Ellis. What she received was a shower of condoms—two hundred or so, she thought, if she didn't count the ones rolling under the bus or scooting off the jetty to splash into the sea.

As a welcome it was spectacular, Susie decided. She smiled with delight, even as she realised it was accidental. The bus driver had hauled out a parcel from between the passengers' belongings. It had resisted, and then suddenly burst open in all directions.

Condoms were flying everywhere.

The cluster of Guides who'd alighted with Susie stared in amazement, and then burst into delighted adolescent giggles as they realised what they were seeing.

'I assume those are mine.'

The voice made Susie jump. It was deeply male and richly resonant, with a lilting trace of a Scottish accent. She turned to find a man climbing from a dusty red Range Rover. His expression was resigned, as if he was accustomed to Whale Beach postal services and this was nothing new.

The condoms were his?

Why on earth would he need so many? Susie's freckled nose crinkled in amusement as she assessed his chances of retrieving them. The chances weren't great. The Guides were swooping on the condoms with shrieks of joy, and their leader was snatching them back with cries of horror. The condoms were everywhere! Including…on her?

Susie put her fingers to her hair and there was a disc resting in her mop of blonde curls. She lifted it free, grinned and handed it over to the stranger.

Who was he? He might be a local, but she didn't know him. Maybe he'd arrived at Whale Beach after she'd left. Whoever he was, he was obviously very needful of condoms. A heap of condoms!

'I don't want mine,' she told him, pressing the foil-covered protection into his hand. 'It's a start, at least.'

He accepted her offering with a resigned and slightly crooked smile. He looked nice, Susie decided as their fingers touched. The stranger seemed thirtyish, or maybe a little older. He was seven or eight inches taller than Susie's five feet four, he was broad-shouldered but with a lean, well-muscled body and he was tanned and weathered in a way that made him look like he spent his life outdoors.

Their fingers kept touching and their eyes met.

He was, in fact, almost breathtakingly good-looking. With a tiny gasp she hauled her fingers back. What was she doing?

No, she definitely didn't recognise him. She might have been away from Whale Beach for four years, but she'd definitely have remembered this outstanding member of the male species.

How could she not? Even as she tried to keep her appraisal detached, she had to admit he was gorgeous!

She took him all in, approving his casual yet smart open-necked shirt and good-quality jeans. His crinkling jet black hair was as dark as Susie's riotous curls were blonde, and his deep grey eyes had laughter lines that sort of made you want to smile right back at him.

He was finding it hard to smile, and the laughter behind his eyes was fading. The man was clearly worried. He'd accepted Susie's condom offering without a word, seemingly unaware of her jolt of attraction, and he was now turning to the bus driver.

'Are the rest safe?'

'You mean there's more?' Susie asked incredulously, and the stranger shot her a withering look.

'The rest of the parcels are safe,' the bus driver told him, hauling extra packages free with considerably more care. Then he couldn't resist asking the obvious. 'They're not all full of condoms, are they, mate?'

'No.'

'There's another one stuck in your hair,' one of the Guides told Susie, and she blinked and foraged for more. Her curls were thick and tangled so they'd have held a good few, and she'd been in the direct line of package fire.

'You'd best give it to the man.' The bus driver grinned at Susie and his glance flickered downward. Which was nothing new. Advanced pregnancy seemed a universal attraction. 'It's a bit late for you to be needing these, love,' he told her.

It was indeed. Susie's smile didn't fade. She reached forward to retrieve her suitcase from the hold of the bus, but the driver lifted it down before she reached it. 'Don't you go carrying that yourself,' he told her, putting it at her feet in the expectation that someone else would help. 'Not in your condition.'

Susie shrugged at that. She had no choice. She might be seven and a half months pregnant, but for the last two years—or even before that—ever since Charlie's lymphoma had been diagnosed, Susie had been very much on her own.

She coped herself, or she didn't cope at all.

'I'm OK,' she told him. 'I've managed this from overseas and I'm on the home leg now. Is there a taxi in town?'

'Only Eddie's minibus.' The driver had stooped again and was collecting all the condoms within reach. He glanced up as the vehicle in question pulled up at the wharf. 'Here it is now, but I'd guess it's already been booked by the Guides.'

'It has.' The Guide leader sniffed and started shepherding her charges minibus-wards, trying to collect condoms from her charges as she went. She wasn't successful. Discs were being stuffed everywhere. For fifteen-year-old girls, this was precious booty indeed.

'The bus is taking us to the Scout camp three miles out of town,' she told Susie, clearly taking pity on her being left with these appalling males. 'I'll send it back for you, if you like.'

'That'd be kind.'

'Or maybe the man with the condoms could give you a lift.' The woman's tone said it was unlikely—he really was a species apart.

But maybe he could. The stranger looked up from where he'd been retrieving condoms from behind the bus's wheels, and he managed a smile. Once again it caught Susie's attention and it held. It was some smile!

'I'm sure I can,' he told her. 'If you don't mind waiting until we've collected these, and if you don't need to go too far, I can give you a lift anywhere locally.'

His smile deepened, and Susie took an almost unconscious step back. Whew! This was a smile to make a girl's heart do back flips.

This was ridiculous! She tossed a metaphorical bucket of cold water over herself and told herself to be sensible. Seven-and-a-half-months-pregnant women were in no position to be attracting strange men. She had no idea who he was—and the man was retrieving two hundred or so condoms!

'I don't think so,' she said cautiously, and she could see by his broadening smile that he guessed exactly what she was thinking.

'Hey, they're not all for me.'

He sounded wounded and she had to fight back laughter.

'That's...very reassuring,' she managed, trying to keep her face straight. The man was an engaging lunatic. 'Are you collecting them for your friends? Or do you just have one special friend to share them with?'

He chuckled. It was a rich, deep laugh that matched his smile beautifully, but he didn't answer her question. Maybe it didn't deserve an answer. 'Um...no. Look, I just have to collect the rest of the mail and then I'm free to take you wherever you want.'

'No,' she said, more firmly than she felt. One part of her wanted very much to accept his offer, but there was something about this man that she didn't trust.

It wasn't just the condoms. It was something about his gorgeous smile...

Charlie. Think of Charlie, she told herself firmly. She was a widow and the thoughts she was thinking seemed almost a betrayal.

But...despite Charlie she was thinking them.

'I'm tired after the bus trip,' she told him, and if she sounded scatty and ungrateful she couldn't help it. She motioned to the post-office-cum-café at the end of the wharf. Its windows looked out over the harbour to the mountain peaks beyond—a view Susie had missed for four long years and a view she'd love the chance to soak in again.

Blaise, the postmistress's golden Labrador, was wagging her tail from the top step. Susie was delighted to recognise her old friend, and also to see that the Labrador was heavily pregnant. Her sense of homecoming deepened.

'Hi, Blaise,' she said with pleasure. The greeting gave her time to gather her composure before she turned back to the stranger. 'Sitting here, waiting for the minibus, will be no hardship at all,' she told him, and received another of those blindingly gorgeous smiles for her pains.

'I guess not. It is fantastic.'

It was. Gandilong Peninsula—an Australian wilderness on Tasmania's east coast—would have to be the most beautiful place on earth, bar none. Susie was so glad to be home she was close to being overwhelmed, by emotion as well as condoms.

'At least let me carry your baggage.' He grinned, and before she could stop him he'd heaved her suitcase up the post office steps and set it beside the placid Blaise. Then he stood and looked down at her, his keen eyes assessing.

'You're sure there's nowhere I can drive you?' he asked, and she collected herself enough to give him a reassuring smile.

'I'm sure. Honestly. Blaise will keep me company.'

The man hesitated, his intelligent eyes taking in Susie's advanced pregnancy, her travel-stained maternity dress and battered suitcase, her weariness and her obvious solitude. It was uncommon for lone travellers to come here, much less heavily pregnant ones without obvious money, and his eyes narrowed in concern.

'You're staying in town?' he asked.

'Yes.'

'And you have somewhere organised to stay?'

She must be a local if she recognised the dog, but why was no one meeting her?

'Yes to that, too.'

So that was that. There was nothing else he could help her with. 'Then I guess I'll see you around.' But there was just the faintest trace of reluctance in his voice, as if he really would have liked the opportunity to assist.

Strangely, Susie was feeling the same. But she didn't need him, she told herself firmly. She didn't need anyone. The past awful years had taught her that.

'I guess you and your condom-bearing friends will be sure to see me at some time,' she told him. 'Whale Beach is hardly big enough to avoid people.'

He heard the inference. His face creased into laughter. 'Much as you'd like to,' he finished for her. 'It's OK, you have nothing to fear.'

'Because I'm in an interesting condition already?' she enquired blandly, touching her very pregnant abdomen. 'How kind. By the way, has it escaped your attention that the condoms that rolled to the other side of the bus are being pecked by seagulls? If I were you, I'd be checking for peck holes for the next few months.'

'Hell!' He left her then, and stalked around the bus. A flock of gulls rose and flew a few yards off to await their next opportunity. 'These aren't edible, dopes!'

'Good luck,' Susie called to him, lifting a hand in a farewell wave. 'Now and in the future. Peck holes can be disastrous.'

'Thank you.' He glared. And then he couldn't help himself. The grey eyes twinkled and he looked again pointedly at her stomach. 'I guess you'd know.'

'I sure do, though it wasn't a seagull that caused this.' If only he knew! 'But you're welcome,' she said cheerfully, and turned her back on the lot of them—Guides, bus driver and good-looking man with far too many condoms.

Good-looking males apart, she suddenly needed to be alone.

Because, welcome or not, she was so happy that she felt like hugging Blaise to her and shouting her joy to the world.

She'd made it. She was home.

CHAPTER TWO

Two hours later the minibus finally deposited Susie at her destination.

Whale Beach Medical Centre, Hospital and Nursing Home were all built as one. The house itself—Susie's home since childhood—was at the end of the long row of connecting whitewashed stone buildings. A verandah ran the entire length, with French windows opening alike from hospital wards, medical reception rooms and the living quarters of the doctor's residence.

It was a beautiful building—and it was home.

But still it was the medical centre. There were cars parked out the front. Clearly her father's former partner, Robert Fraser, was seeing patients and Susie didn't want to face anyone yet. She wanted to get her bearings, dump her gear and take a few deep breaths.

So she carried her suitcase around to where the house yard overlooked the creek meandering down to the sea. This was the doctor's private garden. Her private garden. Susie opened the gate and there was a child in a wheelchair—sitting under her tree!

Whatever Susie might have been expecting after four years' absence, it wasn't this. She pushed the gate wide and it lurched drunkenly on its hinges. That was OK. Robert, the elderly doctor who ministered to Whale Beach's medical needs, had his own home apart from the hospital, so she'd expected a neglected house, but she hadn't expected a child.

She walked cautiously forward, edging back into her territory. The child seemed asleep. Pale and over-thin, the boy was slumped forward with his face resting on pillows. Something was seriously wrong with him, Susie decided.

Something more than a temporary broken limb had immobilised him.

So what had put him in a wheelchair? Her professional curiosity was aroused. He was nine or ten years old, she guessed. He had deep black hair that curled into tendrils and badly needed a cut. Long black lashes fluttered down over his too-pale cheeks, and his jeans and sweater seemed too big for his lanky frame.

Diagnosis? Uncared for, maybe—but what else?

He wasn't paraplegic or quadriplegic, Susie thought, or if he was then the cause must be very recent. His legs still had muscle mass, but there was no plaster cast or brace to indicate a break.

So what was wrong with him? And what was he doing under her tree?

Her tree...

Susie's senses were pulling her everywhere. Distracted, she dropped her suitcase and looked up at the vast eucalyptus casting shade over the garden. The tree sprawled outward, leaning toward the sea. You could see for ever from its highest branches.

Long ago, Susie's father had threatened its removal so he could grow more vegetables, but after his tiny daughter had learned to climb Dr Ellis Senior hadn't stood a chance. The tree had stayed.

Now, looking up through its branches for the first time in years, Susie's emotions were close to overwhelming her. The child in the wheelchair momentarily forgotten, she placed a hand on her very pregnant middle and made her own unborn child a promise.

'You'll climb this, too,' she swore. 'That's why I brought you home, all the way from England. This is where you'll grow up and, despite everything, I know this is what your father would have wanted.'

That was enough! Any more and she'd start to weep, and the time for tears was long over. This was the time for action and for happiness—for setting down roots and getting on with the rest of her life. She closed her eyes, and when she opened them the child was watching her.

'Hello,' he said, and it was evident by his cautious tone that he regarded her presence as an unwanted intrusion.

'Hi.' She smiled, trying not to sound defensive. After all, this was her back yard.

'Can I help you?' The boy was being polite, but his face was wary. Oddly wary. This was a child who seemed afraid of shadows.

'I guess… I'm looking for Dr Fraser.'

'Both the doctors are inside.'

Both the doctors? Susie blinked, trying to make the pieces of the puzzle fit. Robert was the only doctor here, and that didn't explain the presence of the child.

'Is there a queue, then?' she asked cautiously. 'Is this why you're outside—waiting to be seen?' Maybe an anxious mother had pushed him around here for a little peace while she kept his place in the queue.

But it still seemed odd. The doctor's private garden was sacrosanct, and the locals knew it. The child's answer was more puzzling still.

'No. I live here.' His tone added an unspoken rider. You don't. So what are you doing here?

'You *live* here?'

'Yes.' He was about as welcoming as a wet blanket, and he might just have slept but his weariness was still obvious. He sounded exhausted. 'We do. This is private. You'll find the door to Reception around the front.'

'I… Yes. I know my way.' She moved to the verandah and the child's voice cut sharply across the tranquillity of the garden.

'I said Reception is around the front. That's a private entrance.'

'I know it is,' Susie said grimly, and pushed open the back

door. Enough was enough after all. 'I know it's private. After all, it's *my* house.'

Both doctors?

Susie's mind was racing. What on earth was happening? Since her father had died, there'd never been more than one doctor in this town, no matter how desperately Whale Beach needed more. The whole area was desperately short of doctors. This was growing stranger and stranger by the minute.

What was most curious was that there were male voices raised in anger, and the voices were coming from the centre of the building. To be specific, they were coming from the room Robert Fraser used as his surgery.

Susie took a deep breath and walked toward the voices, listening all the way. Outside, the child was bristling in anger, but even though a ramp had been newly built to accommodate his wheelchair, he made no move to follow.

Which was just as well, given the state of her emotions. This was still her house, she reminded herself. No one had permission to be in this section. The rest of the buildings contained the surgeries—one for her father while he'd been alive, and one for Robert. They contained waiting rooms, Reception and beyond them the wards of the small bush nursing hospital and nursing home, but the house itself should have been as she'd left it four years ago.

It wasn't. Someone had added the wheelchair ramps, and there were personal belongings she didn't recognise scattered everywhere. And on the kitchen table were boxes she did recognise.

The condom boxes?

She took everything in as she made her way through to the closed door of Robert's surgery, and she listened unashamedly to the voices as she went.

'Why didn't you tell me?'

It was a male voice—deep and rich and strongly masculine with just a hint of a Scottish lilt. She'd been right in recognising the condom boxes, then. Here was her friend from the bus, but the laughter she'd heard then had disappeared completely. What she heard was fury.

'I've made Jamie promises I can't keep,' the voice snapped. 'The Australian Medical Board will never approve my registration here now.'

'I'm sorry, Darcy.' This was another voice she recognised. Her father's partner was close to seventy, and it was Robert she was coming home to work with. Or…was it?

Robert was still talking. He sounded as if he was explaining—or trying to.

'Darcy, since Susie's father died, I've tried my best to find a new partner,' he was saying. 'No one's wanted to come, and I've been desperate to wind down. The practice really is too big for one doctor, the tourists are increasing and with this post-polio syndrome getting worse, you know I can't cope. I'm getting tired. Susie's always known she'd be more than welcome to work here, but she moved to England with her husband four years ago. He died two years back and she made no move to return. But now… Like it or not, this is her house and it's her surgery.'

'And she writes and says she'll be home any minute.'

'She has the right to be here.' Robert sounded distressed, and Susie's heart went out to him. He'd been under too much of a strain. Val had written that the polio he'd suffered from as a child was causing recurrent problems. She should have come home earlier, she thought bleakly, but it had been such a hard decision. What to do?

Unconsciously her hand crept to her stomach as she listened.

'Darcy, I'm sorry but I can't see what I can do for you,' Robert was saying. 'Your application for rural doctor status here was a bolt out of the blue. I was so grateful. But Susie—'

'Susie has precedence, and I'll never get registration now.' The stranger sounded sick as he heard the implacable note in Robert's voice. 'You know how important it is for me to get residence here, but the Australian government only appoints overseas doctors to areas of need. You had to talk hard to convince them you wanted to wind down. But now… With two doctors here—you and this Susie woman—I'll never be permitted to stay.'

'I'm afraid you won't.'

'So where does that leave Jamie and Muriel? And what about you?' The stranger sounded concerned as well as angry. 'With post-polio syndrome affecting you so badly, you need serious medical help here, Robert. Not someone who thinks half the medical income is her right. This woman's reputation around the town is hardly that of a hard-working doctor.'

'That's not fair.' Robert was on the defensive now, and Susie could understand it. Robert had always been one of her staunchest allies. 'The town doesn't know what Susie's like as a doctor. She hasn't been home for years, and then it wasn't to work. It was to be with her father. Whale Beach has never seen her as a practising doctor, but her qualifications are excellent.'

'They say she's a bit of fluff.' Darcy—whoever Darcy was—now sounded derisive. 'What is she? Twenty-seven? Twenty-eight? And she's already been through one husband.'

'That's hardly fair…'

He obviously wasn't in the mood to feel fair. 'Robert, since I've moved here I've heard one story after another about her, and all I'm hearing is fluff. They tell me she's known as the matchmaking medico, with half the young ones in town saying they owe their relationships to her.'

Out in the hall and still avidly listening, that made Susie smile. So Whale Beach still remembered her. Matchmaking medico? Hmm. Well, maybe she had been at that.

'I'm not disagreeing with you there.' Susie could hear the weary smile behind Robert's words. 'Our Susie's a breath of fresh air, but she does—or did—have a habit of poking her nose into other people's affairs. Maybe if we can think of a way to keep you both here, she'll get you married.'

'Oh, great.' The Scottish accent broadened in distaste. 'As if I need a wife…'

'Why have you never married?' Robert asked curiously, and Susie's left ear promptly flattened against the closed door. Any minute now she could be sprung by a patient or receptionist, and this was none of her business, but she wasn't leaving for the world. After all, this was her house and here was gossip—in her very own surgery!

'As if I have time for women.' Darcy gave a harsh and derisive laugh. 'I learned early to steer clear. My mother deserted us. She walked out when I was five and we never saw her again. My sister stuck around until I was thirteen and then she did the same. Like my mother, she went from one partner to another. The result's outside sitting in that wheelchair, and my sister doesn't give a damn about him. You're not married, are you?'

'No,' Robert said mildly. 'But only because—'

'Because you saw sense. Women! They're all the same. You get attached and they just mess with your life and leave. And here's another one coming to mess us up.'

'Just because your mother and your sister were fickle…'

'And my fiancée,' he said savagely. 'Despite my father's advice, I tried the love bit, but I was a fool. So from now on I want nothing to do with women. Ever!'

It was as good a cue as any. Oh, dear.

Susie took a deep breath, knocked lightly—and opened the door.

Whoa…

At the bus stop, the stranger had seemed good-looking and charismatic. Here, in the closer confines of the surgery with a white medical coat thrown casually over his outdoor clothes, the man was almost overwhelmingly attractive.

She recognised him at once, but if he recognised her he gave no sign. He gave her a blank, cursory assessment as something that might have crawled out of a piece of overripe cheese. His mind was obviously on far more important matters than interfering patients.

'This is a medical meeting,' he snapped, digging his hands into the pockets of his coat and turning away from her. 'Our receptionist is out the front.'

But Robert's reception wasn't so cold. The elderly doctor stared at Susie for a microsecond, and then the walking stick he was carrying was cast aside and he was across the room enveloping her in a vast, welcoming hug before she could say a word.

'Susie. Susie! Welcome home, girl. It's so good to see you. Let me look at you.'

He held her at arm's length and there could be no disguising the joy on the older man's face. It warmed Susie's heart, and it made the unknown Darcy take a step back and stare in confusion.

This was…Susie?

There could be no doubt. Robert was turning the woman to face him and his weary eyes were glowing with pride and with love.

'Darcy, let me introduce my god-daughter and the daughter of my very dearest friend. This is our Susie—or I should say, Dr Susie Ellis. Susie, this is Dr Darcy Hayden.'

She'd had more warning than Darcy. Susie was more collected—sort of. She managed a smile, she held out a hand in greeting, and after an infinitesimal pause Darcy took it.

He still looked stunned.

'*You're* Dr Ellis?' he asked incredulously, and she nodded politely. Warily.

'That's right.'

'I'm…' He took a deep breath, collecting himself. 'I'm pleased to meet you,' he managed. 'Again…'

I bet you are, Susie thought dryly, but she somehow kept her smile in place. His hand was strong and warm and sort of nice. Maybe he was nice, she thought. Just…not nice to her any more. Two hours ago he'd been concerned for her, but now she was in the way of his plans.

'Did you find all of your condoms?' she asked politely, and despite her wariness her eyes danced. 'Or do you need to be frugal for the next week or so?'

But his sense of humour had disappeared completely. 'The local shopkeeper refuses to stock them. They're for the pharmacy we're trying to set up,' he snapped. 'Or...we *were* trying to set up.'

'What do you mean by that? Is there a problem with my arrival?'

One thing Susie had learned over the last two years was that you didn't get anywhere by shilly-shallying. You stated what you wanted, you stated it over and over, and you didn't budge until you got it. Her hand crept to her stomach again. Here was the living proof of that.

'I couldn't help hearing your voices from the hall,' she said, and then watched as both men's eyes followed the protective curve of her hand. 'Robert, has my coming home caused trouble?'

'Nothing that can't be sorted,' Robert said uneasily, his eyes widening as he took in her condition, but Susie had turned again to face Darcy.

'Well?' she said—and waited.

'You're pregnant,' he said flatly.

'Well diagnosed.' A thirty-three-week pregnancy was a bit tricky to disguise. Susie's green eyes twinkled, her humour resurfacing as it mostly did. There wasn't much she couldn't bounce back from.

Not after the hand the last four years had dealt her.

'Yes, I am,' she said, and there wasn't the slightest hint of defensiveness in her voice. Why should there be? She was so proud of this pregnancy.

'And you're proposing to come here and work as a partner to Robert?' Her obvious pride in her pregnancy hadn't deflected him one bit. Darcy's voice was still incredulous, his anger breaking through.

'That was the plan,' she told him. 'But I gather there's a problem.'

'Robert needs a full-time partner!'

Her smile died. 'That's what I'm prepared to be.'

'In between breast-feeding and nappy changes! Ha!'

'Excuse me?' There was no mistaking his anger now—the blatant hostility. He was furious. But he didn't have a monopoly on anger. Susie took a step back and her green eyes flashed. Anger met anger head on. OK, there might be a problem, but she had some rights here, too. Like—this was her home!

But Darcy was giving no quarter. 'Robert needs a full-time medical partner,' he repeated, as if she were too stupid to understand without repeats. 'He's been advertising for a couple of years, and you must have known that. He has post-polio syndrome and he should be winding down. With me here he can do that. We can even expand the practice—like putting in a pharmacy so our patients don't have to travel thirty miles to get their medicines. But now, if I can't stay here, he's stuck with you!'

His disgust was starting to grate. Susie flushed, put her hands on her hips and glared. What gave him the right to judge?

'This is my home,' she said, in a voice so soft it was dangerous. 'The surgery belongs to me. Robert has never bought out the property from my inheritance. He's never wanted to.' She took a deep breath. 'I gather that's your son outside? Am I to assume you're living in my house?'

'Susie…'

Susie's eyes flew to Robert who was looking distinctly uneasy. 'I'm sorry, love, but it all got too complicated,' he told her. 'It seemed easier to let Darcy and Jamie live here, and I couldn't contact you. I've been trying for weeks. I wrote to your English address but it came back unopened.'

'So by just arriving out of the blue you're putting me out of a job and out of a place to live.' Darcy's face looked like thunder. 'Of all the—'

'Inconsiderate doctors?' Susie finished for him, flashing fire. 'That's hardly fair. Robert's been asking for years if I'd like to come home, so I wrote and told him I was coming. Then, when I get here, there's someone living in my house.'

'Your letter only arrived with today's mail,' Robert said unhappily, and Susie faltered in mid-fire. Surely not.

'I sent it three weeks ago.'

'From where?'

Uh-oh. Susie blinked, thinking it through. She'd been upset and frightened, and she'd fled to one of the remotest parts of Scotland while she'd come to a decision.

Maybe the postal system hadn't been all that crash hot, she thought ruefully. And added to Whale Beach's remote status...

'It arrived today, Susie,' Robert said again. He gave her a half-smile that told her he was deeply worried. 'We've only just read it.'

'Oh, heck.' She bit her lip and glanced sideways at Darcy Hayden's thundercloud of a face. 'I'm sorry, but I never dreamed you'd have found another doctor. I've been in Scotland, taking time to think things through. I...I came to a decision there.'

'About your future.' Robert's face softened. 'Susie, you should have told me you were pregnant.'

'I didn't want you worrying.'

There was a pregnant pause. A very pregnant pause. Robert was fighting valiantly to figure out a way to ask, but there wasn't an easy one. Finally he just asked it. He was a family doctor after all, and sometimes it was just easier to bring the hard question into the open.

'Is there a man on the scene?' he asked finally.

Her face tightened. 'No. Not since Charlie died.'

'Charlie being your husband,' Darcy said heavily, and Susie turned and gave him an old-fashioned look.

'Well guessed.'

'I thought he died two years ago?'

'He did.' Her chin tilted as she read the snap judgement in his eyes. 'So what are you saying? You've taken my house and my job, and now you now want to run me out of town with an S branded into my forehead as a scarlet woman?'

'Susie, that's unfair,' Robert said uneasily, and Susie took a deep breath and admitted that maybe it was. A little. A very little.

But he—Darcy or whoever he was—had some explaining to do, and it didn't help that he was looking at her pregnant bulge like it was the product of a scandalous affair.

'So tell me,' she said, forcing herself to count to ten and give the man a chance. OK, if they'd just received her letter this morning, then maybe they were forgiven for using her house. She had told Robert he could use it for emergencies if he ever needed to, and if Robert hadn't known she was coming and had finally found himself a partner...

Oh, heck. This was hard. She needed this job.

'Just tell me,' she said again, and met Darcy's steely eyes full on. 'Why are you living in my house—and why am I messing up your life plans to practise medicine in Whale Beach and sell condoms by the thousands?'

Darcy was forcing himself to count to ten as well. He needed this job. Hell, he'd never needed a job so much in his life. With his medical qualifications, jobs were normally his for the taking, but they weren't for the taking in this wilderness. Like it or not, he was stuck in this place, and this woman was definitely interfering with his plans.

It wouldn't be so bad if she was competent, he decided—if she could do the job—but this pregnant scatterbrain wasn't Whale Beach's answer to its medical needs. He was!

But he was living in her house. She owned the partnership and Robert would come down on her side. That was clear.

So… Talk her out of it, he thought desperately. Maybe even turn on a bit of charm. Tell her how needful he was.

He needed to be persuasive.

'I need to be here because of Jamie,' he told her, and Susie's watchful eyes grew thoughtful.

'Jamie's the little boy outside in the wheelchair?'

'That's the one.'

'And Jamie would be…your son?'

'No.' He was thinking fast as he spoke, trying to figure out the best way to present his case, but his hesitation had her exasperated.

'You need to be explicit here,' she told him. 'Otherwise we'll be here till Christmas.'

'Jamie's my nephew,' he told her. 'He's my sister's child. My sister… Well, Grace is no saint as far as motherhood goes. She abandoned Jamie with his paternal grandmother when Jamie was five, and now no one knows where she is. Muriel—Jamie's grandma—has been doing a first-class job of looking after Jamie, but a few months ago she had a stroke.'

'I see.' Susie didn't but she was prepared to listen. 'Muriel is…?'

'Muriel Barker,' Robert told her from the sidelines. These two were sparking off each other and Robert seemed an outsider—a worried outsider. 'Sam Barker was Jamie's dad before he was killed in a road smash a few years back.'

'I remember.' She did, too, thinking back to the vague rumours of a woman Sam had married and regretted. She also remembered Muriel's steely decision to take on their unloved child.

'Jamie's been pulled every which way. He has all sorts of problems, and now Muriel's in hospital with no long-term chances of taking care of him again.' It was Robert talking now, deeply worried. Trying to make Susie see Darcy's point of view. 'Two months ago, Social Services were saying Jamie needed to go into foster-care and Jamie was desperately unhappy. Apart from his grandma, the only relation he had was his Uncle Darcy who was working as a family doctor just outside Edinburgh. So I contacted Darcy and Darcy offered to take care of the child—back in Scotland.'

'That was good of you,' Susie retorted.

Darcy caught her note of disdain and the thundercloud on his face deepened.

'I happen to like the kid,' he snapped, and she nodded.

'Very uncle-like.'

'Shut up, Susie,' Robert said warningly, and she managed to give him a smile. It was a flash of the old Susie returning.

'Yeah, OK. So we have a concerned Uncle Darcy taking Jamie back to live in good old Scotland. What happened to that plan?'

'Jamie collapsed,' Darcy said, in a voice that took all the humour out of the situation. 'He was nervy as hell to begin with—with parents like his who could blame him? But with Muriel's stroke...'

'He came down with the flu and got pneumonia on top of it,' Robert said heavily. 'From then it's been one thing after another. But unspecific things. He's had swollen glands, he's been throwing temperatures for no good reason, he's getting weaker and weaker, and he sleeps. All the time.'

'We've run a battery of tests,' Darcy interrupted, and he turned to stare out the window, as if he could see beyond into the garden where his nephew was probably asleep again. From this window all you could see was the sea, the lovely bay where whales came in to give birth to their young, but Darcy wasn't seeing any whales. He was looking at a very personal nightmare. 'The paediatricians in Hobart have now classified it as CFS.'

'Chronic fatigue syndrome?'

'Yes.'

'How old is he?'

'Ten.'

Susie frowned. 'That's incredibly young to be suffering from CFS.'

'Young, but there have been instances as young as nine. And Jamie's been under incredible pressure. He's intellectually gifted, he's sensitive and he knew from the start that his parents didn't want him. His gran does want him, he loves her, and he's been desperately trying to take care of her alone because he didn't want her to go into a nursing home.'

'But she had to be admitted anyway, and Jamie's pneumonia triggered the CFS,' Robert added. 'He just didn't seem to get over it. His AST—his liver transaminase—stayed twice the upper limit of normal range, he's had constant sore throats and headaches, and finally he found it impossible to get out of bed. By the time Darcy arrived, Jamie's problems had compounded into a psychiatric disturbance, with him curled into a foetal position. He was almost unable to talk, with no spontaneous conversation at all. If you knew the time and effort it's taken for Darcy to get him back to this stage...'

'He's still far from well.'

'That's what I mean,' Darcy broke in. 'And to move him now... If I can care for him here then he can see his grandmother every day. He can wheel himself through the building to visit her whenever he wants. This place and Muriel are his only constants. Muriel won't shift from Whale Beach. To tear Jamie away without her—to take him back to Scotland with me—is impossible. Like it or not, the kid needs me.'

Susie blinked. This was looking unarguable. 'So you're prepared to work here?'

'Yes. I've been practising family medicine in Scotland, and I have no ties. I came out here, liked what I saw and decided the obvious solution was to care for Jamie here.'

'And you need to work.'

He sighed. 'I'm hardly old enough to retire. This is a long-term problem. I'm not poor but I'm not exactly rolling in money.'

'You can't just stay on a visitor's permit?' Susie was

clutching at straws here. The more she heard, the more she didn't like what she was hearing.

'This is long term and you know it,' Darcy said harshly. 'If you're any sort of doctor at all, you'll know CFS doesn't disappear overnight, and there's still the issue of tearing him away from his grandma. Muriel won't move. We've had enough trouble persuading her to stay in a nursing home, much less leave Whale Beach.'

'So you'll stay here until Jamie's better—or Muriel dies.'

'That was the plan,' he said harshly. 'With Robert's blessing, I'd decided to work here, and until you turned up it looked possible. Under the rural doctor scheme, overseas doctors can apply to practise in Australia, as long as they sign a contract to work for a minimum of two years in an under-doctored place.'

'Which this place was until today,' Robert said. He hesitated, watching Susie's face. 'Do you really want to work here, love? I mean, you'll have a baby to look after soon.'

She bit her lip. This was hard. Back in England it had seemed simple enough, but now, faced with Darcy's dilemma, things were no longer clear cut. 'I need to work,' she told them. 'Like you, Darcy, I can't afford not to earn a living, and here I have a home.' She closed her eyes. 'I'm sorry. If I'd thought—'

'Or let us know earlier,' Darcy said roughly. 'It would have helped.'

'It wouldn't have made any difference at all,' Robert told them. 'The problem's the same. There's hardly a rural community in this country that's not screaming for a doctor. Even though we can use two doctors—heaven knows, I was busy enough when your dad was here, Susie—there are other places where the need is greater. If there's a full-time doctor already working in Whale Bay, or two part-timers—you and me, Susie—then Darcy won't be given rural doctor status unless he moves elsewhere.'

'And Jamie's grandma is here.' Susie stated the irrefutable fact.

Silence. There was nothing to say.

'I guess I could retire completely,' Robert eventually said bleakly, and the two younger doctors stared at him.

'No,' Susie said. 'You don't want to, do you?'

'No, but—'

'But it wouldn't work anyway,' Darcy said shortly. 'You stated your need to wind down when we applied for my registration. As far as Immigration is concerned, I'm eventually expected to be the sole doctor here, and that's why they'll accept me. There are places up and down this coast with no doctor at all. If Dr Ellis here comes back to work, there's no chance of me getting registration to practise in Whale Beach, and there's no chance I'll be able to stay.'

'The whole thing's impossible.' Susie's voice was bleak. She was watching Darcy's face, and she didn't like what she saw. Or maybe she did—and that made the whole thing worse.

But Darcy was still looking at options. 'Look, how much useful medicine are you going to be able to do with a baby anyway?' he demanded. 'Why not take a year or so maternity leave? Most women do.'

Ha! Susie's stomach clenched in envy. Maternity leave? What a luxury! But it was a luxury for women with stable, wage-earning partners, or for women with savings that hadn't been eroded by years of illness-induced debt.

'Because I can't afford it,' she said through gritted teeth. 'I might own this house, but that's all I own. I'm broke.'

'You might have thought of that before you became pregnant.'

Her sympathy for the man's dilemma was fading fast. Any minute now she was going to slug this creep. 'Thanks for the suggestion,' she managed. 'It's almost eight months too late and I don't need it.'

'And you don't need me.' He sounded as angry as she was. 'You expect me just to move on.'

'I don't know what I expect,' she told him. 'Look, can we...?'

Then she paused. The door was opening, and a middle-aged woman appeared from the hall. It was Val, the receptionist who'd worked here since Susie was tiny. Susie started to smile, but Val's eyes registered Susie only for a microsecond. Clearly there were more important things on her mind.

'Oh, Susie, it's you.' But this was no welcome. Her face was shuttered in distress. 'Dr Fraser...Dr Hayden...'

'What is it, Val?' Darcy stepped forward, sensing trouble.

'Kerry Madden's just rung. The haystack's collapsed. Steve Madden and his children are trapped underneath.'

CHAPTER THREE

THE troubles Susie was causing might well no longer exist. Every doctor in the room moved into professional mode, and the change was instantaneous.

'Is there anyone but Kerry already at the stack?' Darcy's voice was curt and incisive, and Val winced.

'I doubt it. Kerry just screamed down the phone that they were all trapped and she needed help, and then she slammed the phone down. I assume she's alone.'

'Then contact the fire brigade,' Darcy told her. 'Get everyone you can there. The first thing is to get the hay lifted.'

'Try the pub, too,' Susie suggested. 'There are always people there.'

'I'll do that.' Robert was already moving to the phone. 'Val, you call the fire brigade and then ring every farm north of the Maddens' starting with the closest. Get every able-bodied person you can. I'll call the pub and the south farms, and I'll set up Theatre here so you can send patients back on need. I'll be here to receive them. Darcy, you and Susie get yourselves out there now. The Range Rover's got most of the gear in and it's only a two-seater.'

'But…' Darcy turned to Susie. 'Wouldn't it be more sensible for Susie to stay?'

'Susie no longer knows who's living where and who to phone,' Robert snapped. 'I'm damned sure Susie can practise medicine as well as me, or better, and it's best if there's a doctor here so if there's multiple injuries you can send minor things back to me and work on. You know that. So go. Don't just stand there, man. Go.'

Darcy made one last protest at Susie taking her place as a doctor. 'I don't know where—'

'Susie knows where the Maddens' place is. Val will take care of Jamie. Stop arguing. Move!'

They moved. Once a decision had been made, Darcy Hayden wasn't one to mess with trivia. Neither was Susie. She'd been trained in emergency medicine. She deferred to Darcy as he knew where equipment was, but she was right behind him, lifting saline bags and IV cradles, snapping open bags and checking drugs were where they were meant to be and gathering any other gear she could see that was clearly needed.

Finally she followed Darcy to the Range Rover with a speed that matched his.

Until a few weeks ago she'd been working in a busy casualty department in northern England and her pregnancy hadn't slowed her down a bit. She didn't falter until the back doors of the Range Rover were slammed shut, they were in the cabin and the Range Rover was roaring out of the surgery car park, Darcy's hand firmly blasting on the horn to warn oncoming traffic of their coming.

'How many kids do the Maddens have?' she said at last, as they turned onto the main road out of town and Darcy relaxed his horn blaring. 'When I was last here there were three but—'

'Five and another on the way,' Darcy said shortly. 'Kerry Madden had her three-year-old in for an earache three weeks ago. She's a sensible mother, but she's tired to death. The three-year-old and the one-year-old have been added since your departure. That makes five kids under twelve years old, and Kerry's pregnant again. And...'

'And?'

He'd paused. It was like he was talking to himself and had to be prodded to keep speaking aloud. Now he flashed her a look that said he'd almost forgotten she was there, but he shrugged and kept talking.

'Kerry's been ignoring this pregnancy. I only just managed

to check her blood pressure and listen to the baby's heart during the toddler's earache check. Her blood pressure was up then. Despite me asking her to have weekly checks, she hasn't been near me since. I've tried contacting her, but I can't get past her husband, and the man just won't listen. And now this! How the heck can this have happened?'

'Steve Madden's not the most intelligent farmer,' Susie told him. 'Or the most caring parent. Kerry was married at sixteen, and maybe he wasn't a particularly sensible choice. She does her best, but when I knew him Steve was almost thirty, he was drinking too much and Kerry was carrying all the load. If she's been busy with little ones... I'd be guessing he'll have pushed the kids to load the trailer, and they've been doing it unsupervised.'

'They'll have been loading from the bottom of the stack because it's easier,' Darcy said grimly. 'Hell.'

'It might not be so bad.' Susie was thinking it through. 'If there's only a few bales...' She paused and thought some more. 'No. Kerry's not one to panic, and she could have shifted a few bales herself. Especially if the kids were yelling from underneath, which you'd think they would be. Surely they can't all be desperately hurt.'

Darcy's grim face tightened even further. 'You think they'll be smothered?'

'If there were only a few bales they could fight their way out,' Susie said. 'Steve's a big man. So I guess we're expecting pressure fractures and internal injuries.' She lifted the cellphone from the console near the gear lever, and cast Darcy an enquiring look. The more she thought about this the more she didn't like it. 'Should I put the air ambulance on standby from Hobart in case we need an airlift?' she asked. 'We can always cancel if we don't need it.'

'Good idea.' He cast her a sideways glance of dawning respect, then waited as she dialled and listed requirements. As she finished, he frowned, clearly puzzled. 'You know the system?'

'I was brought up here, remember?' she said softly. 'My mother died when I was ten and after that I went everywhere with the two doctors. I was literally practising medicine before I went to medical school.'

'They were good friends—your father and Robert?' Darcy had eyes for nothing but the road, but even though their minds were already in emergency mode, there was time to talk of other things. The Madden farm was still three minutes away.

'They were.'

It was good to think of something other than the awfulness ahead. Years of working in Casualty still hadn't hardened her, but now Susie managed a smile, remembering. 'Neither doctor was what you might call a one-eyed medical man. My dad loved gardening and fishing, and Robert loved his painting. Neither was money-hungry. Apart from peak tourist season, they've practised here almost as part-time doctors, and they loved it.'

'We've become busier. The tourist season is practically year-round now, and when your dad died Robert was left alone. You were never tempted to come home?'

'I was…busy,' Susie told him cautiously. 'Robert told me he wouldn't mind working as a lone partner for a bit to save for his eventual retirement. He planned it so it'd be one last burst of hard work and then he'd quit. But then…well, my husband died, and after a while Val wrote and told me just how hard Robert was finding it. As you say, the tourist influx has added hugely to his workload, and now Robert's polio symptoms seem to be returning.'

'They have,' Darcy said grimly. 'It's a damnable disease. He suffered so much as a kid, and now to have symptoms coming back as he ages… It's not fair.'

'No,' Susie said bleakly and she thought of her Charlie. 'Life's not.'

That gained her another curious glance. There were things about Susie that Darcy didn't understand, but he couldn't afford to look too deep. He had things he had to defend. Like Jamie's future.

'So you came home,' he said flatly.

'Yes.'

He cast her another sideways look, assessing. 'But now I'm here. The problem's solved. Robert has help, so you can return to England with a clear conscience. I'd assume after years in England you have a life there?'

'It's not as easy as that.' Damn. It was so hard not to sound resentful. This had all seemed so straightforward—before Darcy.

'Why not?'

She flashed him a glance that said the thing was obvious. 'That's a stupid question. I need to work and who's going to take on a pregnant doctor? The hospital I was working in needs a full-time casualty officer. I can't stay as emergency specialist in a busy hospital and look after a baby at the same time. I'm broke and I need to work full time to support myself. If I keep working in England—or anywhere else in Australia, for that matter—I'll have to put my baby in child care. Here, I have a home and I can use...'

But he was only seeing what was affecting him. 'You're expecting to use Val for child-minding,' he said explosively.

She nodded, refusing to respond to his anger. 'Maybe. If she's willing. Much as you use Val for Jamie now, I'm guessing. Or if not Val, then I can find someone else who can come into the house while I work in the surgery. That's how my father cared for me after my mother died, and as I got older I went everywhere with him. The locals accepted it as normal. If they wanted Dad, they got me, too. It's a perfect set-up.'

'It is.' His hands clenched white on the steering-wheel, and she sighed.

'I'm sorry.' She was at that. She couldn't have been more sorry if she'd tried. He had his needs, but so did she, and they didn't mesh. If she stayed then he couldn't. It was as simple as that—and she couldn't leave.

'We'll talk about it after this,' he said grimly, and she nodded, but she could see no solution. One of them had to go. But the best thing to do was concentrate on medicine, which looked much the easier option at the moment.

'Take the next turn on the left,' she told him. 'The house is half a mile on the right and the gate to the haystack is another hundred yards past the letter box.'

'You know this country like the back of your hand.'

'I should,' she said softly and then added a rider. 'It's my home.'

Kerry Madden was waiting for them, and by the look on her face things were desperate. Her face reflected horror.

It also reflected exhaustion. Not only had she run back to the house to make the phone call, she'd also run the length of the paddock and somehow torn down the fence to allow vehicles through. And she'd done all this while carrying a hefty one-year-old.

Susie squeezed herself into the middle of the seat to make room. The back of the Range Rover was set up as an ambulance, so it was either that or climb over onto one of the stretchers. And Kerry needed attention. As Darcy steered the Range Rover onto the rutted ground between road and paddock, he paused momentarily to allow the woman to clamber aboard. She climbed in, then sagged against Susie in a state of absolute collapse.

'Put your head down,' Susie ordered as Darcy focussed on getting the vehicle to the haystack at the other end of the paddock. 'Now, Kerry.'

The woman was so exhausted she couldn't speak. Susie lifted the child from her arms, pressured Kerry's head between her knees and concentrated on keeping her conscious. The last thing they needed was for Kerry to faint.

Kerry Madden...

Susie had known this woman since childhood. They'd shared a desk at school; they'd been best friends for a while—but things had changed dramatically for both of them.

In her arms Susie held Kerry's one-year-old, and it didn't take a medical degree to tell that Kerry was almost as pregnant as Susie. And although they were the same age, Kerry seemed much older.

She looked worn from child-bearing, she was wearing ripped and stained khaki overalls, her blonde hair was badly in need of a cut and her work-stained hands were scratched and bleeding, as if she'd been trying to haul the haystack apart by herself.

And there were other differences. Worrying differences. Her hands were puffy, and her wedding ring looked far too tight. Looking further, Kerry's face was swollen and it wasn't just from crying. Her eyes were set back in cheeks that Susie was more accustomed to seeing in patients who'd been on steroids—not healthy young pregnant women.

There was more to be concerned about here than the accident, Susie thought, but the accident was all Kerry was worrying about.

'I can't find any of them,' she gasped while Susie still held her head down. Her face was ashen, she could hardly speak and her lip was bleeding from where she'd bitten it. 'None. Oh, God. None.' She took a searing breath, fighting for words to explain the unexplainable. 'Half the stack's come down.'

As Kerry fought to sit up again, Susie put her arm around the woman's shoulders and held her, hard. She willed her strength into Kerry as she stooped to talk with her. 'Take your time. Tell us what's happened.'

Another jagged breath. Kerry's fear was raw and almost palpable, and above her head Susie and Darcy exchanged concerned glances. There were medical needs right here. They'd have liked to have stopped now and attend to her, but there was no time.

'Come on, Kerry. You can do it.'

And she did. Somehow, although her voice was a thready whisper with no strength behind it at all, Kerry raised her head from her knees, gazed sightlessly though the windscreen and started to speak.

'Steve sent the children out this morning to load the trailer—like he has every day this week,' she whispered. 'It's school holidays, you see, and Steve said it was time they helped, even though I worried. I've been so tired with this pregnancy I haven't had time to go down and check like I normally do. But Steve said it was fine. Anyway, Steve took the truck to meet them a couple of hours ago. He attaches it to the trailer when they've finished loading, you see, and they go round the cows together. But then none of them came home for lunch.'

The child in Susie's arms stirred and fretted. Kerry reached out, and the woman's stained and scratched hands stroked the baby's hair in a gesture of instinctive comfort. Susie had an almost unbearable urge to do the same to her.

'Then...' Kerry forced herself to continue. 'Then I waited and waited, until Daniel woke...' she gestured to the baby '...and we walked over the paddocks to find out what was keeping them. And half the stack's fallen.'

Her breath sucked in at remembered horror. 'Oh, God... It was so high. They must have been pulling from underneath. The truck's there—it's still by the haystack—but the trailer hasn't got any hay on it and Steve's not there. Or he's underneath. He must be. And the keys...the keys must be with him. I had to run back to the house and it's so far...'

Her voice faltered and her words ended on a shattering sob. Susie's arm tightened around her shoulders, instilling what comfort she could.

'Hang on, Kerry,' she told her. 'Help's on the way. We'll have every adult in the district here within five minutes and the stack will be pulled apart before you know it. And the hay's not too heavy. Just think the best.'

'Oh...' She could barely take in what Susie was saying,

but somehow she thought that through. 'How? I only phoned the surgery before I ran back.'

'Val and Dr Fraser are phoning everyone they can think of to get them here.' Susie hesitated. The Range Rover was still lurching across the paddock, but already she could hear the screaming of the fire engine approaching from a distance. She glanced back and the road was filling with a stream of cars. 'Here comes the cavalry.'

Kerry glanced back, saw what Susie was talking about and for the first time her eyes seemed to focus. She turned back to Susie, her eyes widening. 'You mean it.' And then her eyes widened further. 'It's…it's Susie Ellis. Our Susie.' Finally she realised who she was talking to. Until now there hadn't been room in her terrified thoughts for recognition of her old friend. 'I didn't know you were home.'

'I always come home when I'm needed,' Susie told her, and her voice was filled with foreboding. 'Or maybe when I'm not needed. Let's just hope I'm not needed now.'

She wasn't—or not in the way she'd thought.

Within two minutes there were twenty vehicles surrounding the mass of collapsed hay, and there were more able-bodied men and women shifting hay than could possibly be needed to haul the stack apart. Susie was left on the sidelines.

The stack had collapsed at one end. One half was still standing, but the other was a vast, jumbled heap of broken bales. Grant Dobson, Whale Beach's fire chief, took charge. Darcy moved in to help haul bales, but before he did, he ordered Susie to stand back and wait with Kerry.

'Kerry's under enough pressure without this,' he told Susie in an undertone. 'Just look at her! It's my bet her blood pressure's sky-high. I was worried about her before this, and with the exertion she's undertaken she's risking this pregnancy. All the signs are of advanced pre-eclampsia. It'd be best if you could get her back to the house.'

Susie shook her head, knowing such a demand was impossible. There was no way she could make Kerry leave. It was all she could do to stop her throwing herself at the bales again.

'I'll stop her doing anything physical, but it's useless to try and get her away from here. She stays,' she told Darcy. She met his eyes directly, and the man had enough sense to accept what she said. Kerry was immovable.

'Then get my bag from the truck, check her blood pressure and make her sit. I don't want her going into shock.' He glanced at the woman's swollen face, and his expression tightened. 'Or worse.'

And he could see from Susie's face that she knew exactly what he was talking about. Susie wasn't stupid.

But Susie was frustrated. Kerry refused point-blank to leave or to sit, or even allow Susie to check her blood pressure. She stood like she was frozen, simply staring at the stack, watching as Grant and Darcy took charge.

'I want no more pressure from the top,' the fire chief was saying. 'No one climbs. We're taking out bales from the sides, and we're reinforcing as we go.' He frowned as his volunteers started work. 'I can't understand why no one's making noise from underneath. The hay's loosely piled, and there's no vast mass bearing down.'

'It's heavy enough,' Darcy said, giving Susie another silent message to keep Kerry clear—to move her so she couldn't listen—but Grant frowned again and continued.

'Yeah, it could crush a kid, but a bale falling against a man is another thing. It'd be unlucky if it completely crushed him, and if it moved sideways there'd be an airlock. And even if Steve was unlucky... We're talking five people here. And why is the trailer empty? If Steve came up here and found the kids buried then he wouldn't be underneath himself.'

'Kerry said he came up an hour or so after the kids.'

'Then the kids should have put a fair bit of hay on the trailer before he got here.' The fire chief was still thinking it

through. 'The other possibility is that they all went around
to feed the cows, came back to load for tomorrow and then
got into trouble, but that doesn't sound like our Steve. Never
do anything today that can't be put off until tomorrow is our
Steve's motto in life.'

He shook his head, and motioned his people to work. He
had no more time to waste on idle thought. 'OK. All we can
do is dig, but be careful.'

'Watch for air locks,' Darcy ordered the volunteers. 'Move
slowly, and act like it's a game of pick-up-sticks. You only
move a bale if you're sure you're not causing more bales to
move, and I mean that. Work in pairs and hold everything
steady. I want no more damage than has already been caused.
Go!'

They went. Practically the whole adult community of
Whale Beach seemed to be there now, and within twenty
minutes they'd shifted every bale until they reached the section of the stack that hadn't collapsed.

And they found no one. Not one body. Not one injury.

No one.

All that time, Susie had been standing on the sidelines,
holding onto Kerry—or maybe Kerry had been holding onto
her, and holding as if her life depended on it—but as the
bales cleared to the section that was still neatly piled and the
workers stood back, confused, Kerry's frozen control finally
snapped. She broke into jagged, tearing sobs and fell to her
knees. Susie knelt with her.

'Oh, God. Where are they? Where are they?' At the movement of every bale, Kerry had been waiting for the worst.
As the last section had been checked she'd practically
stopped breathing and now there was no explanation. No
bodies. Just…nothing.

And then there was a yell, sounding faintly from the far
side of the Maddens' land. Someone looked up, someone
yelled a warning—and there was Steve Madden striding
across the paddocks toward them.

He was walking as if there were nothing wrong in the entire world, and he was followed by four children. Susie stared, and then put her hands on Kerry's heaving shoulders, turning her to see.

'Kerry…'

But Kerry was past noticing. She was dry retching onto the ground. Susie waited until the worst had past, and then lifted her chin and forced her eyes to where the trail of children was growing clearer all the time.

'Kerry, stop it. There's no need for tears. They're on their way to us right now. They're safe.'

The woman didn't move from where she was kneeling. She lifted a tear-stained face and stared at her approaching family, but she didn't make a sound.

Neither did anyone else.

Silence.

What could have been a cry of triumph from the searchers didn't turn out that way. From across the paddock the Madden kids were speeding up as their father led them back to the stack. They were clearly fascinated by the presence of the fire truck and the crowd, but every person who'd been involved in searching was staring straight at Kerry.

Kerry's swollen face was now blank and pale with shock, and her eyes were disbelieving. She didn't say a word, but with Susie's help she staggered to her feet. Darcy moved to her other side, his face mirroring Susie's concern.

'Dear God,' Kerry whispered. At her feet, one-year-old Daniel was cooing and murmuring and grabbing handfuls of loose straw, as if he didn't have a trouble in the world, but not so his mother. 'Dear God,' she repeated. 'They're…they're all here. Safe. My babies.'

'They're all safe, Kerry.'

But it was finally too much.

'I'll kill him,' she whispered, and then her legs sagged from under her, her eyes rolled back in her head, and if Darcy and Susie hadn't been holding her tight she would have ended up on the ground.

'I don't see what all the fuss is about.'

Steve Madden hadn't changed one bit. Not a bit. Susie remembered him as a charming, good-looking male who'd got more than one girl into trouble before he'd finally married Kerry. It seemed his sense of responsibility hadn't improved with his marriage. Now, even though his wife was semiconscious on the ground, he was busy explaining his actions to the fire chief, and his voice said he was astounded that all this fuss had been made.

He'd got flabbier over the years, Susie thought. He had the look of a man who spent too much time with the bottle and not enough time on hard physical exercise. He certainly didn't look like a farmer.

'I came over to help the kids and the stack collapsed just as I got here,' he said petulantly, noting the looks of accusation all around him. 'Lucky the kids weren't under it. So I thought, damn, it's going to take days to rebuild, and I'd worked enough this morning. So we fed the cows and I took the kids for a swim. The river was great. I knew as soon as I got back to the house Kerry'd be on about rebuilding the stack, so I thought we might as well enjoy ourselves before she started carping on.'

'Kerry'd be right. There's rain coming and the hay needs to be covered,' one of the local farmers said heavily. 'You're a fool, Madden. You always have been.'

'You can butt out of my business, McGregor.' Steve Madden's face flushed crimson. 'Look, if Kerry's gone overboard and panicked.... And now she's fainted. Well, that's a woman for you. Hell, she might have known I wouldn't be stuck under that lot. It'd take a bigger stack than this to kill me.'

'It could have killed you,' the fire chief said, his eyes contemptuous, and then he moved deliberately away to where Susie and Darcy were working on Kerry. 'Is she OK?' Like

Steve, he'd assumed she'd simply fainted, but this was much more than a faint.

'No,' Darcy said. Kerry hadn't lost consciousness completely, but her muscles had gone into spasm and she was gripping Darcy's hand like she was drowning. Susie was fitting a blood-pressure cuff over her arm as Darcy organised an oxygen mask. They'd worked in tandem since she'd collapsed, each anticipating the other's needs, and they were working fast. Darcy spoke roughly to the fire chief but his attention was totally on Kerry. He flashed an enquiring look at Susie and she shook her head. Instinctively he knew she was as worried as he was.

'A hundred and sixty, a hundred and ten,' she said, and he winced.

'Her blood pressure's sky-high—hell, we're moving into eclampsia territory here. This isn't a faint. She's fitting. If we can't get her blood pressure down we're risking a stroke.'

'Eclampsia?' The fire chief looked a question.

'High blood pressure. Dangerously high blood pressure. It can cause fitting or a stroke and that's just the start of it. Hell, if we don't get it down... Steve, I *told* you she should be having bed rest, and why on earth...? Grant, can you clear the way to the Range Rover and bring the stretcher across? And radio to the air ambulance. We already have them on standby from Hobart, but tell them we need them urgently and we need a neonatal team on board.'

'A neonatal team?' Steve's attention was finally caught. 'What—for the baby, you mean? No way. She's only six months gone.'

By his side his oldest child, a little girl of about eleven, was standing looking like her world was falling apart, but he ignored her completely.

'I warned you...' Darcy stated.

'She'll be all right as soon as she gets her breath back,' Steve interrupted uneasily. 'This is only a stupid faint. Hell, she might have known we'd be safe. Of all the damn fool things to think!'

'She thought it,' Darcy said heavily. 'But that's past. Let's just concentrate on keeping your wife and baby safe.'

'Safe! Hell, Kerry's not in any danger, is she?'

Susie looked around the crowd of volunteers and made a swift gesture to a woman she recognised. It was understood. The woman stepped in, lifting the little girl away from her father. 'Come on, love,' she said, 'Let the doctors look after your mummy.'

And with the child gone, Darcy could finally say what he wished. 'I told you weeks ago,' he snapped. 'Her blood pressure was rising then. I wanted weekly visits, and Kerry needed rest. I wanted her in hospital then for a complete check, but you wouldn't hear of it, and now you pull a stunt like this. I explained—'

'You didn't!'

'You wouldn't listen,' Darcy said heavily. 'But you're listening now.' He motioned to baby Daniel who was busy stuffing straw into his mouth, and then to the distressed little girl. 'I suggest you look after your son, Mr Madden. Look after all your children, in fact. Follow us into the hospital as soon as you can. We can't wait for you. Dr Ellis and I are going to need every bit of luck we can get—and then some— if we're to save your wife.'

Kerry had her second major convulsion in the back of the Range Rover and it was far worse than the first. From semi-consciousness, her body started jerking in rigid muscle spasms, and she slipped into complete oblivion almost immediately.

'I'm not surprised,' Darcy said heavily, pulling to the edge of the road as Susie rolled Kerry onto her side. One of the firemen had come with them and Kerry's small body was so swollen that it took their combined strength to roll her. 'I'm coming back in there,' Darcy said. 'Henry, take over at the wheel, and take it slow.'

Then he was in the back with Susie, organising equipment and fighting to keep Kerry still. The roads here were rough and unsealed, and injecting under such circumstances—and in such cramped conditions—was something Susie wouldn't have liked to try, but Darcy had obviously done it before.

'I should have gone out to see her,' he said, half to himself and half to Susie. 'Three weeks ago I was worrying about her blood pressure and now, with this swelling, she'll be lucky not to have a major stroke.' He was injecting intravenous diazepam, but his set face told Susie he knew the uselessness of what they were doing. They could do so little while they still had to worry about Kerry's baby. The diazepam dose he could give to a pregnant woman wasn't nearly enough.

And Kerry's baby was so far pre-term....

She should be down in Hobart right now.

'The raised blood pressure was only mild three weeks ago?' She was guessing, but Susie had seen enough of Darcy's caring to know he wouldn't have sent a woman with pre-eclampsia home.

'Yes.' His voice was rigid with anger and Susie could tell that some of that anger was directed at himself. 'Although, as I said, I couldn't do a complete check. Steve was waiting and she wouldn't stay for more than a couple of minutes. As I told you, she was more worried about her toddler than herself. I rang a couple of times and got Steve. I talked him through the pre-eclampsia threat—told him I was worried— but he assured me Kerry was fine. He was helping and she was getting plenty of rest. He can be...persuasive.'

'He's always been that.' The Range Rover had slowed to almost a crawl. The local police car was giving them an escort, its blue light flashing in front, but the need for speed was less than the need for immediate treatment. Darcy had located the vein and set up an intravenous line almost as easily as if they'd been in a casualty cubicle.

But Kerry was still rigid on the stretcher, her body arching into spasms and never losing its awful rigidity. Her convulsion was lasting way too long.

'How are you at emergency Caesars?' Darcy asked grimly, and Susie winced.

'How many weeks did you say?'

'Twenty-six.'

'Darcy, there's so little chance…'

'Of a viable baby? I agree. Not if we deliver it at Whale Beach, but unless the air ambulance is available right now—which it hardly ever is—then I don't think we have a choice. We'll lose Kerry if we don't get this baby out.'

'But—'

'Susie, the neonatal team will be here as soon as possible, and we'll have to depend on them to increase the baby's chances of survival. If we can keep it alive that long. We—you and I—though, can't think of that. If we wait then we lose both mother and baby. We go in now and concentrate on Kerry.'

'Darcy, I don't think I can.'

He cast her a hard, uncompromising look.

'Robert seems to think your medical skills are up to scratch. You can give an anaesthetic?'

'Yes, but not like this.' All Susie felt was panic. 'I've never given an anaesthetic for a woman as ill as this. I have general training. This is specialist anaesthetic territory.'

'And it's specialist obstetrician stuff. Unfortunately I don't have a specialist obstetrician and I don't have a specialist anaesthetist. I have you and we have Robert. If you can't do it then Robert must, and your hands don't shake as Robert's have started to do.'

Darcy fixed her with a look that allowed no argument. No matter what he thought of her as a person, he needed her now as a doctor, and everything else was put aside. 'Robert will have to be the one to cope with the baby if the neonate team doesn't arrive on time. We'll radio ahead and tell him to set up Theatre for emergency Caesar. As soon as we get back I'll telephone for specialist obstetric advice, but I don't think that advice will give us a choice.'

'Darcy, no.' But she knew the protest was futile.

'Welcome to the medical world of Whale Beach, Dr Ellis,' Darcy said grimly. 'This is what you wanted. This is what you've got!'

CHAPTER FOUR

SEVEN hours later, Susie finally had time to sit. Seven hours...

They'd been some of the longest hours she'd ever spent, she thought as she slumped into the armchair in the kitchen at the rear of the house. And they'd failed. Three doctors hadn't been enough.

It hadn't been for want of trying. Darcy was a fine doctor, she'd discovered. He'd been amazingly skilled at surgery and he was someone she'd be content to rely on in most emergencies, but this had been an emergency that had needed a city hospital, a full obstetric and neonatal team and luck thrown in for good measure.

It hadn't happened. The plane with help had been delayed for too long to wait. Darcy and Robert and Susie had pitted every ounce of their medical skills against the odds, but the odds had been too great.

The result? One Caesarean. One tiny baby boy who'd lived only minutes, despite their desperate attempts to save him, and one desperately ill woman who'd been transferred by air to Hobart, still convulsing.

Kerry would be lucky to live, Susie thought bleakly. At least now that she was no longer pregnant, the medical teams could concentrate solely on her survival. In the intensive care unit of Hobart's main hospital she had a chance but, dear heaven, at what cost?

Steve, still blustering but sagging around the edges, had gone with the air ambulance, accompanying the flying medical staff and Kerry to Hobart. Robert was coping with evening surgery and Darcy had returned to the farm where Kerry's parents were taking care of their grandchildren. His

48

job was to take them the news, and try to explain the unexplainable.

Both jobs would be terrible, Susie thought grimly. Robert's and Darcy's. Every patient in the district would know about the tragedy by now, and Robert's job of answering the locals' questions would be almost as bad as Darcy's.

Sometimes being a doctor was the pits, Susie decided wearily, and ran her hand protectively over her own abdomen. Please, God, that such a nightmare not touch her...

'The baby died.'

She glanced up. Here, in the big, open-plan kitchen that had been her home for ever, Susie had slumped down in the armchair by the stove like one who was completely at home. She'd forgotten it was also home for ten-year-old Jamie.

'Yes, Jamie,' she said gently. 'We did everything we could, but sometimes everything's not enough. The baby was too little to be born, and it died.'

He nodded, with a look that was over-wise for his years. 'Uncle Darcy will be sad.'

'I guess a lot of people will be sad.' She watched as the small boy pushed his wheelchair across to the kitchen table. He was so serious. So...

Hardened, she thought suddenly. He was a child who expected the worst, and he expected it because the worst always happened. His mother abandoning him. His father dying. His grandmother having a stroke.

And now here was Susie, coming to tell him his uncle couldn't stay here with him. She knew full well what it meant. If Jamie wanted to stay with Darcy then he'd have to return to England and leave his grandmother. What sort of a choice was that for a small boy to make?

'Val says to tell you there's a casserole in the oven,' he told her. 'I've already had mine, but there's heaps for you and for Uncle Darcy when he gets home.'

'Thanks.' She wasn't hungry but, heavily conscious of the new little life within her—and how fragile it was—she forced herself to go through the motions. To spoon out a plateful of casserole and eat it while the small boy's eyes watched her every move.

'I've been to see Gran,' he said at last, and she nodded.

'Your gran's in the nursing home?'

'It's right next to the hospital,' he told her. 'I can wheel myself there from here. Gran likes seeing me a lot, and I go at least twice a day. It's easy from here.'

He paused then, as if he had something very important to say. And finally it came. 'I told Gran you'd come back,' he said tightly. 'And she said...she said if you'd come back to work then my uncle can't stay here and I'll have to go away.'

Oh, no. Susie thought back to what she remembered of Jamie's grandma. Muriel Barker had always been as sharp as a tack, and it seemed her stroke hadn't deprived her of any of her mental faculties.

'We need to sort that out,' she said. 'We'll talk about it over the next few days.'

'Gran says if you work here then the government won't let Uncle Darcy work here, too. Is that right?'

She swallowed, but there was no way out of this. 'Yes.'

'But you can't work and have a baby,' Jamie protested. 'You have to look after it. You can't be a doctor, too.'

'I can.' She sighed. 'Many women must work when their babies are tiny, and I'm one of them. I can't afford to do anything else, Jamie.'

'But if you work, what happened to Mrs Madden might happen to you.'

She smiled, trying to be as reassuring as she could—which wasn't very reassuring. 'I won't work that hard. I promise.'

His mouth turned mutinous. 'But it's true. Gran says if you work here then Uncle Darcy will have to leave, and they'll make me go with him. I asked Dr Fraser. He says the only reason they're letting my uncle stay in Australia—working here—is that Dr Fraser wants to retire and Whale Beach won't have a doctor without him.'

'Jamie—'

'Dr Fraser says Uncle Darcy might get a job further along the coast.' The child's words were increasingly desperate. 'But it's thirty miles at least to the next town. They'll make me stay with him. I know they will, and I know he won't bring me to see Gran every day. He won't have time.'

'Jamie, I can't—' But there were no counter-arguments.

'If my uncle goes, I'll stay here by myself,' he said furiously. 'You can't just come and kick us out.'

'Jamie, this is Susie's home.'

The voice from behind made Susie start. She'd been so intent on the small boy's fury that she hadn't heard Darcy enter. Now she turned to find him standing wearily at the door.

His face was haggard. What he'd had to face—explaining to the Madden children that there was no new baby, and explaining to Kerry's parents just what Kerry's chances were—must have been dreadful.

And now this! He'd come home to face Jamie being evicted from the home he'd pinned his hopes on.

The knowledge almost overwhelmed her. This big-hearted man who'd come half a world to give his nephew a home, who'd cradled a dying baby with such tenderness that Susie had wept—this man who'd taken on the responsibilities for the medicine of this town—was now being robbed of everything by her.

But there were other things on her mind as well. Dreadful things. 'Kerry?' she said softly, and waited with a hollow feeling in the pit of her stomach for the verdict.

'I've just been in touch with Hobart. She's stopped convulsing for the moment and there's no evidence of stroke, so that's our one piece of decent news for the day. It's early yet, though.'

Susie nodded. Eclampsia couldn't be controlled until the

baby was born, but even after the birth there were often days or weeks of danger.

'We can only hope. And Steve's with her?'

'The hospital staff told me when she finally regained consciousness Steve was nowhere to be found. Out, getting drunk, I expect.'

'Oh, no! Poor Kerry.'

'She should kick him out,' Darcy said savagely. 'The locals tell me it's her parents' farm—not his. I can't understand why she doesn't.'

'Maybe she loves him.' Susie gave a bleak, wintry little smile and then turned back to Jamie who'd been soaking in their conversation like a sponge. 'Like your uncle loves you, Jamie. Coming all the way from England to care for you.'

'My grandma loves me,' Jamie whispered. 'No one else does, and now I have to go away. Dr Fraser says this is your home and I can't stay here any more.'

It was too much. 'Jamie, I'm not sure it is my home any more,' she said softly, and she saw Darcy's eyes widen. 'When I decided to come home I didn't know your uncle was here. Maybe I need to do a rethink. For tonight, though, we're all very tired. I need to sleep and then maybe we need to make some decisions in the next few days. But for now let's not worry about the future.'

'I'm worrying.' Jamie glared.

'So are we all,' Susie told him. 'We need a solution, but for now, even more importantly, we need bed.'

Bed was fine. Bed was easy. It was sleep that wouldn't come. Susie lay in the darkness in the bedroom she'd slept in as a child and stared up at the ceiling for hour upon hour.

The baby's death weighed heavily on her. No matter how much she practised medicine, unnecessary deaths always left her feeling sick at heart, and it was even worse now that she could empathise so strongly with what Kerry had lost.

She'd take better care of her baby, she promised herself,

but the more she thought of her future and the care she could give to her little one, the more she didn't like what she was seeing.

But she had so few options left. She had no money and she had to work. She'd walked away from the home she'd been offered in England and the fury she'd left still reverberated in her ears. She couldn't go back now.

But...neither could she stay. How could she evict Darcy and Jamie from this town?

How could she not? The baby was stirring within her, and the knowledge that she was totally responsible for this new little life was threatening to overwhelm her. The thought of the afternoon's events—of one tiny baby struggling vainly for life in Darcy's caring hands—made her dilemma seem even worse.

She had to give her little one a future. She must. She'd gone into this pregnancy with her eyes wide open, but now things were such a mess.

Sleep was impossible. Finally, in desperation, she pushed back her covers, threw on her robe and slippers and made her way through the quiet house.

Darcy was sleeping in her parents' room. Jamie was in the little room beside it—that was sensible as it meant if he needed his uncle he only had to call. Blessedly it meant also that they'd left her room as it had been.

But Susie didn't want her bedroom now. She wanted a cup of tea and somewhere to think—anywhere where she wasn't reminded of Darcy and his problems.

She padded through to the reception area of the doctors' surgeries. This was peaceful enough. But it was dark and lonely, and beyond were the lights of the little hospital. There was another need added to her list. Company. Life! She only had to go through the door and she'd be back in a medical world. Back where she belonged.

She looked like an escaped patient herself, she thought ruefully, and then thought, What the heck. The staff on duty during the afternoon's drama had all been familiar faces. They all knew she was back home, and the hospital kitchen would be warm. And she'd been lonely for so long...

She pushed through the dividing door. It swung shut behind her, and then snapped open again. She turned—and collided with Darcy, barrelling through behind her.

Because she'd turned, they met head on. He grasped her by the shoulders or she would have fallen.

Unlike her, Darcy was fully dressed. He hadn't been to bed, she guessed. His eyes were dark with fatigue, and his face shuttered as he took in her appearance.

More problems, his look said, and as she looked up at him Susie's heart wrenched in sympathy. She knew instinctively that he'd been going over and over the events of the afternoon, asking himself the same stupid question.

What could they have done differently to affect the outcome?

He was a caring doctor, she told herself as she looked up at him. A good man. To come all this way and make the decision to live in such an out-of-the-way place as Whale Beach for an ailing nephew. She felt so sorry for him. And there was something else she felt.

What?

This was stupid, she told herself fiercely as she tried to suppress the strange emotions she was feeling. Why was she reacting like this to Darcy's problems? She had enough of her own, she knew, but the chemistry between the two of them—this thing she was feeling as he held her shoulders—was there, whether she liked it or not.

'What's wrong?' His harsh voice barked the demand as he automatically steadied her. She blinked up into his concerned face. Darcy was in doctor mode, and he was assuming she was in trouble.

Well, she'd asked for that, she guessed. She was pregnant, she was in pink spotty pyjamas and a blue spotty dressing-gown, and she was in the hospital. Her eyes creased into involuntary laughter. Maybe he was right to assume she was here as a patient.

But he was too tired to see the laughter. 'Susie, what is it?'

Heck, he had the capacity to throw her right off balance, in more ways than one. The caring in his voice, and the feel of his hands on her shoulders as he steadied her... It did strange things to her—things she wasn't sure how to cope with.

'Nothing,' she said, and her voice was surprisingly defensive. 'I thought I might make myself a cup of tea.'

'We do have a kitchen in the house.'

We. The word was weirdly intimate.

'I know,' she managed. 'I didn't want to wake you.'

'As you see...' He looked down at his fully dressed self and gave a rueful smile. 'I'm already awake. And Jamie won't stir. It's as much as I can do to wake him in the day-time.'

'You've been called back?' She pulled away from his hold and, suddenly aware that his hands were still on her shoulders, he also pulled back with a hastiness that said he should have done so earlier. If he'd thought of it.

Or if she hadn't felt so soft under his hands...

She knew Darcy had felt what she was feeling. She could read it on his face. Somehow Susie watched with detached interest as he hauled himself back into doctor mode, forcing his voice to be formal as he answered her question. What was it that she'd asked? Had he been called back?

'Yes.' He motioned to the beeper on his belt. 'A drip's packed up. Laura Hendy had her appendix out this morning. She's a fit little ten-year-old and will probably be OK without the extra fluids, but I figured, what the heck, I couldn't sleep anyway.'

'You operated here this morning?' That didn't make sense. Robert's hands were no longer steady enough to give an an-aesthetic.

'Ian Lars is the closest doctor to Whale Beach,' Darcy told her. 'He practises at Stony Point sixty miles north. We have a deal. I travel for his minor surgery requirements and he travels for my anaesthetic needs. That way patients can stay in their own hospitals. He came up early this morning to help me with Laura.'

'And in emergencies?'

'You've seen today what happens in emergencies,' Darcy said flatly. 'But it's the best we can do.'

'You need two doctors.' She fell silent. 'You must! Is Robert so incapacitated that he can't operate?'

'Yes.'

'And you're on call all the time?' The set-up here was puzzling her.

'Yes,' Darcy said briefly. 'As you know, he lives apart from the hospital and he can't cope with unbroken sleep. Heaven knows, he's suffering more than he lets on.'

'From the after-effects of the polio?'

'It's a damnable thing,' Darcy told her. 'From what he lets on—which isn't much—he suffered enough as a kid. He tells me he spent years in calipers and now, in his late sixties, as he's contending with arthritis and general aging, back comes the polio to haunt him. He doesn't want to give up medicine altogether. He loves living in this town, but there's very little he can do apart from straight consultation.'

Susie bit her lip, and Darcy nodded, knowing exactly what she was thinking.

'It's too much for you to take on,' he told her. 'You never expected full-time practice, but that's what you'll be getting if you stay here. Robert wants to stay in touch but, as you saw this afternoon, he's only too ready to stand back and let someone else take over. He coped with this afternoon's dramas and he did evening surgery but now he's exhausted. It's been too much for him. He can't be on call, and you need to know that.'

'I suppose so.' She faltered and bit her lip again. This was too hard. What was she getting into? She desperately needed time to think this through, and she didn't have it. Decisions were being demanded of her now.

'You need to see your patient,' she told him. At least then she'd be alone to clear her head.

'Do you want to come with me to see Laura?' he asked unexpectedly, and as her eyes widened he smiled, and there was a trace of sympathy behind his grey eyes. 'At a guess, you're roaming around, looking for company and there's company waiting. Laura will be delighted.'

She looked a question at him, and he smiled again, breaking the tension. 'You look worried,' he told her, softening still more. 'I know I've made things impossibly hard for you. The feeling's mutual, but for now maybe we need to call a truce and get Laura sorted.'

'You don't mind if I come?' She looked down at her py-jama-clad figure and managed an uncertain smile. 'I'm hardly dressed in doctor mode.'

'You look just fine to me,' he said, and it surprised her how his assessing eyes had the capacity to make her blush. 'I don't know why I don't wear the same. We could make it standard wear for doctors on night duty. Spotty pyjamas. Very sensible.'

'It might be sensible but it'll hardly make Laura think I'm professionally competent.'

'I suspect what Laura needs isn't doctors but attention,' he told her. 'A pyjama-clad diversion is just what she needs.'

'It's not what you need, though.'

'Maybe I do,' he told her. He shook his head and the look of uncertainty deepened in his eyes. 'Heaven knows, this is one hell of a mess I've got myself into. I've not been awake working until now. I've been up pacing the floor, trying to thing of a solution. Of any solution. I was almost glad of the call to take my mind off it.'

Laura was delighted to see them. The ten-year-old was

sitting up in bed, receiving visitors with all the aplomb of a
senior member of the monarchy. There was a nurse with her.
The nurse rolled her eyes at Darcy as he entered, then looked
curiously behind him to Susie, but Susie hadn't time to be
introduced before Laura started talking.

'I just wiggled my arm a little bit, Dr Darcy, and the drip
came loose,' the child announced, her blue eyes limpid with
innocence. 'The bipper started bipping, and Nurse Carrie
came and sighed and said she'd have to get you to replace
it. Were you asleep?'

Her voice indicated she didn't mind if he had been. This
was a much more satisfactory state of affairs than sleeping.
Then, like the nurse, her eyes moved to Susie. Satisfaction
faded and her voice became accusing. 'Ooh. I know who you
are. You're Susie Ellis, Dr Ellis's grown-up doctor-daughter.
My mum says you've come home to stay and you're making
my Dr Darcy go away.' She glared straight at Susie with full
ten-year-old indignation. 'And that means my friend Jamie
has to go, too, and my mum thinks that's terrible.'

How fast did news travel around this district? Susie wondered grimly, but she dredged up a smile.

'Nothing's been decided other than I've come home,' she
told Laura. 'I hope you don't mind if I help with your drip
tonight.'

There was a dramatic sigh.

'I expect it'll be a good thing.' Laura lay back and put out
her hand with a theatrical little flourish. Darcy lifted it and
started lightly tapping for a vein. 'I expect I'll have to get
used to you. A lady doctor.'

'There's nothing wrong with lady doctors,' Darcy told her.
He found what he was looking for, the nurse handed him the
syringe and he slipped the needle back where it was needed.
Laura sighed again. This time her sigh wasn't quite so theatrical and a tiny tremor in her voice said that the pinprick
had hurt. She really was a sick little girl, and it was the
middle of the night.

'I know there's nothing wrong with lady doctors,' she whispered. 'But I like my Dr Darcy...'

So did Susie.

By the time they had Laura settled, leaving her with Nurse Carrie for company until she went back to sleep, the notion was firmly rooted in Susie's mind. She'd thought it already but here it was, spoken aloud.

I like Dr Darcy...

And he was skilled! This community had been blessed by finding itself a wonderful doctor, she thought, and Susie was under no illusions as to the service she could give to replace Darcy. Twenty-four-hour call, seven days a week? No. She couldn't do it. Not with a newborn baby to care for.

Yet if she stayed, Darcy would have to leave. She thought back to the times her father had pointed out the difficulties the small towns around them had in attracting doctors. Whale Beach was fortunate, but other towns weren't.

What had Darcy said? The closest practising doctor was sixty miles away. That meant there were at least three closer towns without doctors at all. There was no possibility the government would allow a foreign doctor to set up practice here if Susie intended to practise herself.

And if Whale Beach had no Dr Robert, and they replaced Dr Darcy with Susie...

It was starting to look untenable in more ways than one.

They emerged from the ward into the corridor and she found Darcy was looking down at her, a question in his dark eyes. 'Penny for your thoughts?'

'What?' She was caught off balance. 'I guess I wasn't thinking of anything.'

'Liar. You were thinking you can't do it.'

'I don't have much choice,' she said blankly. 'I must.'

Anger flared, surfacing through weariness, and he snapped. 'You could always try returning to England—maybe even to the father of your baby.'

Oh, right. Her eyes closed at that, the ever-present pain rising to the surface. What a stupid thing to say. As if she could. She opened her eyes again and found Darcy still watching her. The anger had gone, to be replaced with the instinctive sympathy she was growing accustomed to.

'I'm sorry,' he said softly. Damn him, she knew he'd seen her pain. 'That was a foolish thing to say when I don't know your circumstances.' Then his gaze grew more intent, seeing past the surface light-heartedness she'd so carefully acquired over these last awful years. 'Are you in real trouble, Susie?'

She gazed helplessly up at him and there was nothing to give him but the truth. 'I'm in all sorts of trouble,' she agreed. 'For both of us.' She hauled herself together and managed a wan smile. 'But it can wait for morning. You can go to bed now.'

'I wish.' He glanced toward the nurses' station, and the charge nurse was grimacing and beckoning him over. 'Ha. I thought so. This looks like more work. Never mind. You go get your cup of tea and go back to bed, Susie, and leave me to it.'

'But—'

She got no further before she was interrupted.

'Darcy, Muriel Barker needs you.' The charge nurse, a middle-aged woman Susie recognised as Lorna Touldbridge, a friend from years back, had emerged from behind the desk to cut across their conversation. She shot Susie a brief smile of recognition. 'Hi, Susie, love. Welcome home.' Then she turned back to Darcy and her eyes were troubled.

'Darcy, they've just rung across from the nursing home. Muriel's distressed, her blood pressure's sky-high and they're worrying about her stirring herself into another stroke. Apparently Jamie's told her what's happening and she's worrying herself sick.'

'Damn.'

Susie winced. Here was more trouble down to her. 'This is my fault,' Susie said grimly, and Darcy nodded.

'It is, but there's not much you can do about it. I should have made time and talked to Muriel myself tonight. It's my responsibility.'

He was responsible for Jamie's grandma, too? He had Muriel's health on his shoulders? Susie shot Darcy a look of deep concern. He'd been pulled from carefree bachelorhood to this? He had the weight of the world on his shoulders and here she was, causing him nothing but grief.

It was looking more and more as if her decision couldn't wait until morning, she thought bleakly. Susie wasn't having another stroke for Muriel laid to her account.

'Let me talk to her,' she said urgently, and Darcy shook his head.

'That'll only upset her more.'

'Darcy...' She laid a hand on his arm and let it rest. 'I know Muriel. I can reassure her.'

'You can't reassure her.' He gazed down at her hand resting on his white sleeve. Gently he lifted it away and let it drop. 'This is an insurmountable problem, Dr Ellis.'

'Maybe. But it's a problem of my making. I need to see her.'

'Susie—'

'Let me try.'

'I don't know.'

'Darcy, I'm a doctor,' she told him. 'I'm not about to cause a further rise in her blood pressure. If I didn't think I could do some good, I'd leave it to you. I promise.'

He gazed at her for a long, unseeing minute, and it was Lorna who broke the silence.

'Let her try,' she urged. 'The one thing our Susie is renowned for is solving other people's problems. She's been doing it since she was four.'

'There's nothing you can do here.'

'Let me try.'

*   *   *

Muriel was in her seventies. Susie remembered her as a fine-looking, big-boned woman, but now she seemed to have shrunk. The stroke had diminished her, and the news she'd had that afternoon had made matters infinitely worse. Her eyes were swollen from weeping. She lay huddled in her bed, and the look she gave Darcy as they entered was despairing.

And Susie couldn't bear it. She hadn't wanted to say the words so soon, but they came out anyway. As soon as she walked into the room and saw Muriel's distress, she knew she could leave it no longer.

'Muriel, I won't do this to you,' Susie told her, before the door had even closed behind them. She crossed to the bed and took the woman's leathery hands in hers. This woman had worked so hard all her life. She'd taken on the care of her grandson without a protest, she'd loved him to bits and it wasn't fair that she should be torn from him now. 'I don't know what the rumours have been, but you're not to worry. I won't take Darcy and Jamie away from you. I'll get a job down the coast and take myself off, but I will not tear you from your grandson.'

There was deathly silence in the room as the old lady took this in. There was silence, too, from Darcy. She heard his swift intake of startled breath—and then nothing.

'Do you mean it?' The woman's voice was a thread of a whisper, hope flaring as she gazed up at Susie. Her eyes said she knew exactly who Susie was, and she knew exactly what she was promising.

'I mean it.'

'Oh, if you only could…'

'I can.'

'Muriel, we need to talk this through,' Darcy said at last. He walked across to the bed and took the old lady's hands from Susie. 'You've been getting yourself into a state.'

'Yes, because I thought…' The woman's eyes were still on Susie. 'I should have known you wouldn't do this to us, Susie, love. You always were a kind child.'

'I'm not a child any more,' Susie told her, trying to cut the tension. She gazed pointedly down at the bulge beneath her spotted dressing-gown. 'As you can see.'

'I can see.' A troubled expression swept across the old woman's face again. 'Jamie said you need to be here. This is your home. It's not right that you can't come back.'

'I can come back. At weekends. On my holidays. I'll get a job down the coast. There's any number of towns needing a doctor, so stop worrying this instant.'

She picked up the blood-pressure cuff and turned enquiring eyes to Darcy. 'Do you want to play doctor here or shall I?'

'I think I'd better,' Darcy said grimly. He took the cuff from her and slipped it on Muriel's arm. 'Not that we need it. I suspect after what Susie's just said your blood pressure will go down all by itself.'

'*If* she means it,' the old lady said, doubt still in her eyes.

'Of course I mean it,' Susie said indignantly. 'Have you ever known me to tell lies, Muriel Barker?'

'No, child, I haven't.' Muriel sighed and lay back on her pillows. 'But it's time you stopped taking troubles of the world onto your shoulders. To leave your home with a little one on the way... It's time you thought of your future.'

'I'll do that,' Susie promised. She stooped and kissed the wrinkled old forehead and then slipped from the room before Darcy could say a word.

I'll do that...

How was she going to do that?

Susie made herself a mug of tea and took it out onto the back verandah of the house. She no longer wanted company. She was feeling almost as bleak as she'd felt in the weeks following Charlie's death.

All her plans. They'd been pointless. She'd been unrealistic. Thinking she could just walk back here and everything would be the same...

She sat down on the back step and gazed forlornly out

over the creek toward the sea beyond. A wallaby was nibbling the grass by the creek. While Susie stared, a tiny joey twisted and tumbled from her pouch, then started nibbling the grass between his mother's paws.

'She's taking better care of you than I can of my baby,' Susie said grimly, and fought hard to stop useless tears welling behind her eyes. She wasn't going to cry. She wasn't!

But at least the joey had a home, and a mother he could be with all the time.

'Mind if I join you?'

Darcy's voice was so soft that she didn't jump. She nodded soundlessly and he came to sit on the step beside her. Jamie's wheelchair ramp took up half the wide steps. What was left was a narrow strip just wide enough for both to fit, and Darcy's broad shoulders brushed the soft flannel of her gown as he settled beside her.

The warmth was somehow threatening, piercing the armour she'd so carefully built around herself over the last two years. She flinched and he felt it.

'Susie…'

'Leave it,' she said bleakly. 'There's nothing else to be said. You and Jamie can stay here. You must. So much depends on it.'

'And you?'

'Like I said, I'll get a job in a town along the coast.' She gave a rueful laugh as she thought of what lay ahead. 'There's no problem in getting a job. I'll charge you rent for this house and that'll pay for child care. See? I have it all sorted.'

'You had it all sorted.'

'I didn't. I should have let Robert know months ago that I was coming home.'

'Why didn't you?' His voice was soft and infinitely caring, and once again Susie felt the piercing of her armour. He sounded as if he cared—and no one did. She knew that now. The caring made her want to cry.

Crying would be stupid!

He was waiting for her to answer, and emotion achieved nothing. Talking achieved nothing either, but maybe he wouldn't condemn her so much if he knew.

'I thought...I thought somewhere else was home,' she told him.

'Somewhere in England?'

'Mmm.' She nodded. Out on the lawn the joey was growing braver, moving a good two feet from his mother. She concentrated fiercely on the two creatures, and tried desperately to block the feel of Darcy's sleeve against hers. His body against hers...

'This baby,' he probed, breaking the silence. 'Do you want to tell me about it?'

Why not? There was no secret.

'This baby is my husband's baby,' she said into the semi-darkness. 'Charlie's baby.'

'But—'

'From Charlie's frozen sperm.'

'I see.' And maybe he did. Maybe he knew the fight she'd undertaken to be inseminated with Charlie's sperm. Even if he didn't, his voice softened further, with a caring that was her undoing. 'Would you like to tell me about Charlie?'

Yes. She would. She'd been silent about Charlie for so long. There'd been sympathy for the first few months, but now it was as if he'd never existed. Except for her pregnancy...

'Charlie was a physician,' she said softly into the dark. 'A good one. He came to Australia six years ago to take a registrar job, but mostly just to see Australia. And to get away from his parents a bit. We met, we married and I followed him back to England. It was supposed to be happy ever after for everyone.'

'But?'

'But three months after our marriage we discovered he had

lymphoma.' She paused but there was no comment from Darcy. He knew as well as she did what such a diagnosis would have meant, and the fact that Charlie had died meant there were no questions to be asked.

She felt his concern, though. The warmth from his body seemed to intensify in the darkness, encouraging her to continue.

So she did.

'When Charlie first learned his diagnosis—before he had his first dose of chemotherapy—he had sperm frozen. We talked about it and decided it was only sensible if we were to have children after he recovered. Only, of course, he didn't recover. Then, when it was clear that he wouldn't make it, he asked if I'd still have the courage to have his child.'

'Oh, Susie...'

Darcy's words were a whisper of sympathy and the warmth she was feeling grew by the minute. Dissipating the bleakness of what she was saying.

'I couldn't do it straight away,' she told him. 'Charlie was right in doubting my courage. I wasn't brave enough. I missed him so dreadfully, and it was all I could do to keep putting one foot after another. We'd been living on his parents' estate in Yorkshire and working in a Leeds hospital, so I kept on working—only harder. I threw myself into my work with everything I had. But I couldn't forget how much he'd wanted a child to follow him...'

'So you want the baby for Charlie.'

'I want this baby for *me*,' she said fiercely, folding her hands over her stomach in a gesture of what seemed almost defiance. Out on the lawn the wallabies looked up, startled, and wallaby and joey instinctively moved closer together. Susie lowered her voice.

'I had to be sure, though. To have a baby, I needed security—a home—and, as I said, the one I had in England was part of Charlie's parents' estate. It seemed right at the time to bring Charlie's baby up in Charlie's part of the world.

So I talked it through with his parents, and to my surprise they were delighted.'

'Why to your surprise?'

'They didn't like me very much,' she admitted. 'They'd wanted an aristocratic English daughter-in-law and I was about as far from that as you could get. A yokel from down under. After Charlie died they treated me as if it was all my fault, so when I broached the idea of a baby I was stunned when they gave me their support.'

He thought that through. 'So what went wrong?'

'I had too much support,' she said bleakly. 'I had support, all right, but as soon as they were sure the pregnancy was well on its way and I wasn't likely to miscarry, I had so much overwhelming support that it scared me to death.'

'You need to explain that to me.'

No wonder Darcy was a good doctor, Susie decided, staring out into the dark. If he used this tone to his patients they'd tell him anything. They'd bare their souls to this gentle, sympathetic man, and she was no exception.

'Lord and Lady Fitzgerald suddenly realised they had an heir,' Susie said bleakly. 'Or heiress. It made no difference.'

'I still don't understand.'

'Neither do I,' Susie admitted. 'It was weird. Frightening. I knew they were strong people. Charlie had to fight to achieve independence, but their attitude to me and my baby was beyond anything he'd ever said about them. I can only think their son's death put them past reason. Anyway, they started laying down rules. My baby would be brought up as Charlie had been raised. I could live in our house as they'd promised—they wouldn't kick me out—as long as I obeyed the rules.'

'Rules?'

'I wasn't to interfere with the child's upbringing. I could work as much as I liked—as I said, Charlie and I had been working in a hospital in Leeds before his death—but the child would have a nanny chosen by them and would be brought up to inherit the estate. It seems that even though they disliked their son, the thought of the estate going to some distant cousin was dreadful.'

'But you're the baby's mother,' Darcy said thoughtfully. 'You have rights.'

'Yes, I have rights, but I don't have any money. Charlie was fiercely independent. We lived in a house on the estate because he loved the place and stood to inherit, but apart from that he had little to do with his parents. When he was ill they didn't help at all—they just wouldn't concede that he was dangerously ill—and by the time he died I was badly in debt. He badly wanted to die at home, you see, and he needed twenty-four-hour nursing. It cost heaps.'

'I can imagine.'

'I'd only just cleared those debts when I got pregnant. But I'd made the stupid, stupid mistake of assuming I was welcome to stay living in our house. I was wrong. I was only welcome as long as I agreed to their conditions.'

'And those conditions were unacceptable.'

'As you say.' Susie's voice was as cold as ice. 'I still had to work in Leeds, and according to the financial conditions they laid down I'd have had to pay rent so I'd have needed to work full time. I'd have seen less of my baby than I would have if I'd used a commercial créche and I'd have had no say in its upbringing.'

'Oh, Susie…'

'I was alone, in a foreign country, pregnant and with these very powerful people threatening to take over my baby. I knew Charlie wanted his child to live where he'd lived, but I also knew Charlie would have hated his parents having control. They're so cold. I was so frightened.'

'So…'

'So a friend I worked with knew the trouble I was in, and he had a cottage in a remote part of northern Scotland. "Go sit by a loch and think about it," he said, so I did. And there I decided if I stayed in Charlie's country, the only alternative was for me to leave the area, get another job and have the baby cared for commercially while I worked to pay for that care.'

'Which is the same alternative you're facing now.'

'As you say. But at least it's *my* country. For me, it's home, even if I need to work thirty miles away.'

Silence. It stretched on and on in the still warm night, endless in its portent.

And then Darcy sighed.

'Susie, you need to stay here.'

'So do you.'

'If it was just me, you realise I'd walk away,' he told her. 'I never would have come here in the first place. But Muriel and Jamie have brought me here, and for their sakes I need to stay.'

'I know that.' He'd come half a world for the sake of one small boy, and Jamie wasn't even his son. How could Susie destroy that sort of commitment?

More silence. Out on the lawn, the joey tired of grass, slithered back into its mother's pouch and nestled down for the night. For some reason, the sight still made Susie want to cry. The wallaby's baby was safe, and her own baby wasn't. She'd made such plans for this baby, and now they were all useless.

Silence.

'The crazy thing is, this place needs two full-time doctors,' Darcy said at last. It was as if he were talking to himself. 'Robert deserves to be able to practise as little as he wishes, but with the increased tourist influx, even with me working full time, he's not able to back off. And there's no pharmacy. Patients have to order in drugs and it takes overnight to get them here. That was the story with the condoms. We hoped to set the pharmacy up, even though I knew we'd be stretched to capacity.'

'Oh.' The syllable sounded flat and hopeless, even to her.

'In fact, this place could use all of us.'

'The government will never agree to it,' Susie said.

'No. I had enough trouble convincing them Robert was desperate for help. Maybe if my two-year rural doctor visa had already come through…but it hasn't. I'm operating on temporary registration. My application for rural status still has to be processed and if you want to work we can't disguise you being here.'

'No.'

But suddenly something was whirring in the back of Susie's mind. Some germ of an idea…

'Susie, I'm sorry.'

'Don't be.' She cut him off, then rose and walked over to the trunk of her beloved gum tree. This idea she was having took some thinking through. Her mind was working in overdrive. Maybe it could work for both of them. If she had the courage…

Would Charlie mind?

No. He wouldn't. She knew that. Not if it meant his child was protected and loved as he'd want it to be.

So all she had to do was tell Darcy what she was thinking.

Whew! She took a deep breath and then another. Courage was something she'd never lacked, but this took maybe more courage than she'd ever needed in her life.

'There is one other way,' she said slowly.

'One other way of what?'

'Of getting you immigration status. Of you being permitted to work here. Of all of us being able to work here together.'

Darcy stared out at her in the moonlight. Blonde, with big eyes and diminutive, Susie looked almost ethereal—a fairy at the bottom of the garden.

A very pregnant fairy, wearing spotted pyjamas…

Despite himself he couldn't suppress a grin and she saw it. She put her hands on her hips and glared in indignation. 'There's no need to laugh,' she retorted. 'This is a very serious proposition, and it just could work.'

'How could it work?'

'You could marry me.'

CHAPTER FIVE

As a conversation-stopper, this was a winner. Darcy stared at Susie for a long, long moment, and then he stared some more.

'I have to assume you're joking,' he said at last.

'Why would I joke about something as important as this?'

'I don't...' His voice trailed off. The man looked like Susie had just thrown a bucket of ice water over him and he was only just resurfacing.

Well, then, she had to present her logic before he made it to the surface.

'If it was just for me I wouldn't think of it,' she said urgently. 'It's not. Maybe, if my logic is right, then it's a solution for all of us. For Jamie and Muriel and for Robert and for my unborn baby. And for you and me.'

'But you don't want to marry me.'

'Of course I don't.' The very idea was ridiculous.

Wasn't it?

'And I certainly don't want to marry you.'

His solidness steadied her. 'That's what's so perfect,' she said proudly. 'If I thought for one minute that you were interested in marriage for real then I wouldn't consider it. But...' she had the grace to blush '...I overheard you talking to Robert. You're not the least bit interested in marriage and I've already been married. I have no intention of remarrying for love, so we make a perfect pair.'

'Husband and wife,' he said faintly.

'Exactly.' She beamed. She was back in organisation mode now, and organisation was what she did best. 'Australian doctors can work wherever they want and, married to me, you'd qualify for citizenship. As far as immigration goes, it's wonderful. Our story's brilliant. We met in England through our common bond of the people we knew in Whale Beach. When Muriel fell ill, you came out to work here and look after Jamie, and I realised how much you meant to me. So I pined for you.'

'Pined?' His voice was disbelieving.

'Pined,' she said smugly. 'I'm very good at pining. I was wafting toward a decline so you rang me up and told me to come home, and as an aside you popped the question.'

'Oh, right.' He looked at her closely. 'You know, somehow I don't see Immigration swallowing the pining bit.'

'Why not?'

'Just a feeling.' The twerp actually grinned!

And maybe he had a point. Pining had never been her strong point—even when Charlie died. 'OK, I'll have refused to come home with you when you first asked,' she said equitably. 'Being a spirited lass with a good job and all. You can be the one who pined, and I can finally have felt so sorry for you that I just had to come. Anything for a quiet life. Don't you see? It's brilliant.'

'Sit,' he said suddenly, and he himself sat on the dilapidated garden seat under the tree. He motioned to the spot next to him and Susie had the sudden impression that this was how he'd humour a deranged patient.

'Hey, it's a good idea,' she said indignantly. 'It could work.'

'Tell me how it could work.' Once more, he was pacifying her.

'For a start, we could all stay in Whale Beach,' she told him. 'As my husband—as the legal spouse of an Australian citizen—you can live and work wherever you want. The Medical Board is starting to get tough with practice permits but they won't separate married couples. Especially when there are kids involved. And the more I see of this place, the more I figure we could use three doctors. You have Jamie to look after and you don't want to be run off your feet with work. I have my baby, and Robert has his health to consider. It could suit us all beautifully.'

He looked at her for a long, long minute, and his eyes widened. 'My God, you mean it!' he said incredulously.

'Of course I mean it.'

'Robert said you were a matchmaker but this takes the cake! You'd seriously marry me?'

She chuckled. 'Well, maybe not seriously, but at least legally. Yes.'

'Did you say we could all live here?'

'We must.' She was thinking things through as she spoke, but she knew there was no other solution. 'This house is big enough to hold us all, and immigration officials will want to check. In everyone's eyes we'll need to appear married. The only person who'll know anything different will be Robert, and I'm sure he'll support us. It's my guess he may even be delighted.'

There was a long, long pause. She looked uncertainly up at his hooded face. 'Darcy, it could work.'

'Yes, Susie, it could work.'

Her eyes creased in astonishment. 'You mean you agree?'

'No,' he said. 'I don't.'

'Why not?' She rose and put her hands on her hips, daring him with those luminescent green eyes. 'Darcy, it's brilliant.'

'It's loaded with potential disaster.'

'Like what?'

'Like who would you say was the father of your baby?'

That floored her. She stared down at him in astonishment. 'Why, Charlie, of course. I wouldn't want it any other way.'

'You'll tell that to Immigration?'

'Darcy, I'm not springing a paternity suit on you here. We met just after I got pregnant. We can work out something.'

He sighed. 'Susie...'

'What?

'Go to bed.' He rose and put his hands on her shoulders, looking gravely down into her eyes. 'This isn't a split-second decision. We're talking marriage here. It involves all sorts of things, none of which you've properly thought through.'

He paused, and the feel of his hands on her shoulders sent warm shivers through the length of her body. He did the most amazing things to her, just by touching her.

She had to force her voice to work. Heaven knew, her mind wasn't working so something had to. 'But we need to make a decision,' she managed. 'The need is urgent.' Her voice had lost its sureness. There was a tremble behind her words that could have been weariness—or it could have been desperation.

Darcy heard it and his voice softened even further. 'We need to sleep on all of this.'

'You seriously think I can go to bed and sleep?'

'I think you need to try, or you'll tumble over with weariness,' he said softly. He put a hand to her chin and lifted her face so her eyes were meeting his. Then he bent and kissed her very lightly on the lips. 'You've had one hell of a day, Susie Ellis. I think this is about the most amazingly generous offer I've ever heard, but it involves all sorts of complications.'

'It's not just for you, you know,' she said, trying for asperity. 'I get something out of this, too. I can't work here on my own. It's taken me less than a day to realise that. Robert's too ill to be a full partner, and if I have a baby to care for then I can't work full time. I need a strong partner, and that partner's you. You're too good a doctor for me—or for Whale Beach—to give up.'

'Gee, thanks.'

She pulled back a little and—reluctantly—his hands released her.

'OK, we'll sleep on it,' she managed. 'Or we'll try. But don't write it off as impossible. It might just work.'

'It might at that,' he agreed gravely, and smiled. His smile in the moonlight was tender and warm, and for some stupid reason it almost made her weary knees buckle.

She looked at him for a long, long moment—and then she turned and fled as fast as her wobbly knees could take her.

Breakfast was very, very strained.

Jamie was at the table first. He was busy buttering a piece of toast; he looked up as Susie entered the room and his face shuttered down in pain.

'Go away,' he said.

'I'm not going to,' Susie told him. She was dressed in elastic-waisted jeans and a pale blue windcheater that reached almost to her knees. It didn't make her look like an efficient doctor—in fact, it made her look extremely pregnant and extremely cute. Despite himself, Jamie's attention was caught, and he left off his toast-buttering.

'When's your baby due?'

'In seven weeks.'

'Is it a girl baby or a boy baby?'

'I don't know. I'm not one for testing something that doesn't matter.'

'Don't you want to know?'

'Nope. I'm waiting to be introduced at the proper time.'

He seemed to approve of that. Then his remembered pain washed back and he went back to fierce toast-buttering. 'I won't be here to find out anyway.'

'You might be,' Susie said cautiously. Whatever happened, they seemed destined to see a bit of each other.

'You should be.'

Damn the man. Darcy had a habit of sneaking up on her like a ghost. Susie turned to find Darcy standing in the doorway, surveying them both.

'You might knock or something,' she muttered. 'You scared me.'

He smiled at that. 'Somehow I doubt if you scare that easily. And as for knocking... You're taking proprietary rights to your kitchen, then?'

She considered. 'Well, it is my kitchen.'

'It is.' He watched as she placed a piece of bread in the toaster. 'But that's my bread.'

She glowered. 'You want me to buy my own?'

'Not if you let me enter *your* kitchen.'

It was too much. The whole thing was ridiculous. She grinned. Her toast popped up, she buttered it and bit into it, and then waved magnanimously to the opposite chair. 'OK, Dr Hayden, you can come in. You can even share our breakfast table. The toast's very good.'

'Jamie and I pride ourselves on our toast,' he told her. 'Don't we, Jamie?'

But Jamie was looking suspiciously from one to the other. 'What's going on?' he asked, and for the first time the dragging fatigue had faded from the little boy's voice. 'Did you say...? Uncle Darcy, did you say I should still be here when Susie's baby is born?'

'It could be arranged.'

The boy laid down his toast and cocked his head on one side. 'How?'

'Susie might marry me.'

There was complete silence in the room for about two minutes while all present took this on board. Susie went on munching, her mind in overdrive. She was acute enough to know, though, that it was Jamie's reaction that mattered here. Darcy would be doing this for Jamie, so without his acceptance the plan was useless.

More than useless.

Marriage to Darcy...

For the first time, Susie took it on board as a real possibility. Last night it had been a spur-of-the-moment idea. Now, in the cold reality of morning, it seemed nothing but crazy.

But Jamie's first reaction wasn't that it was crazy. The child stared at them both for a long moment, and then decided he needed time to think about things. He wheeled his chair over to the sink and concentrated fiercely on making himself hot chocolate. It needed all his attention.

He did it while Susie tried hard to concentrate on something other than the man who'd just made this extraordinary proposal. Darcy sat down in silence, fed his bread into the toaster and waited for some reaction.

He didn't get one. In the end it was Darcy himself who had to force the issue. Who had to speak…

'Well?' he said. Jamie had his back to him and it was impossible for either adult to tell what he was thinking.

'Well, what?' Jamie was playing for time.

'What do you think of the idea?'

The boy turned his chair. His eyes went to Susie, then flitted to Darcy and then rested back on Susie again. 'You…you'd marry each other,' he said at last, and his intelligent mind had figured it out. 'You'd do it so we could all stay here?'

'That's right.'

Jamie's hesitation had given Susie time to get her emotions under control. This was a good idea, she told herself. It must be.

So act like it. Lighten the situation…

She twinkled at Jamie. 'I can tell you're amazed that someone would actually *want* to marry your uncle!'

'I'm not such an ogre,' Darcy started, but Jamie wasn't to be distracted by humour.

'When did you think this up?'

Darcy flashed an uncertain look at Susie, and she gave him an imperceptible nod. It was his call, her nod told him. He knew his nephew better than she did, and he'd know what to say. But she'd seen enough of the child to know that deceiving Jamie probably wasn't on the cards. He was too intelligent to be fobbed off with a story of an old romance.

So it was truth or nothing, she thought, and it seemed Darcy thought the same.

'We thought of it last night,' he admitted. 'But we can't say that to anyone but you. And maybe Robert and Muriel.'

'Why not?' Jamie was fascinated.

'Because Immigration won't let me stay unless Susie and I can convince them we've planned on marrying for ever.'

'You'll say that?'

'I won't lie unless I have to,' Darcy said seriously. 'But for you…'

'You mean you'll marry Susie so you get to stay here all the time. Just for me.'

'That about sums it up.' Darcy grinned down at his too-serious nephew. 'I know it's a sacrifice, but you don't need to feel incredibly grateful.'

'No.' Jamie, his face immeasurably thoughtful for one so young, turned to face Susie again. What he saw seemed to reassure him. There was no trace of a smile in his eyes. He was figuring the whole thing out for himself, and what he saw in Susie's face seemed to reassure him. 'It wouldn't be just for me,' he said at last. 'Marrying Susie would be OK for you, too. She's quite nice. And she's pretty. Even if she is fat.'

'Gee, thanks.' Susie's warm eyes sparkled and, amazingly, Jamie managed a smile in return. 'What a compliment!' she told him. 'You think I'd make your uncle a suitable wife?'

'I think you'd make a nice mother,' Jamie responded, and it was impossible for Susie to miss the note of wistfulness in his voice.

Whew!

Susie took a deep breath as more implications of what lay ahead unfolded. But if this was to work then she had to go all the way. From this moment, they had to live together as a family.

'I guess I sort of will be,' she told him, and intercepted a startled look from Darcy. 'Your uncle's your guardian,' she told him. 'If I were to marry him, I suppose that'd make me your guardianess.'

'That's like...like a mother?'

'That's right.' She flashed another glance at Darcy and saw he was thinking exactly what she was thinking, That there were implications all over the place here—for all of them.

Jamie was still into the mechanics of the whole operation. 'So this baby would be my sort of brother or sister.'

They were going way too fast, but there was no drawing back now. Not with those huge eyes watching every move. 'That's right,' Susie told him.

But Darcy was thinking fast. He could see the eagerness appearing on Jamie's face, and eagerness hadn't appeared on Jamie's face for a long, long time. He intended to make use of it.

'This is all conditional,' he said sternly, and Jamie turned his attention to his uncle. He flinched, as if he was about to have something snatched back from him.

'Conditional on what?'

'On you.'

'On me?'

'On you firstly acting like we're a family—because if we don't do that then Immigration won't let me stay.'

'I can do that,' Jamie said cautiously.

'And there's more.' Darcy had the undivided attention of both Susie and Jamie. Susie was as fascinated as Jamie was.

'It's also conditional on you agreeing to change doctors— and follow doctor's orders.' Darcy was pressing home his advantage for all he was worth, and Susie blinked.

'You mean...' Jamie was off balance. 'Not go to the doctor in Hobart?'

'Only occasionally from now on. I want your new doctor to be Susie.'

That had Susie's eyes widening. Whatever she'd been expecting, it hadn't been that.

'I'm not a paediatrician,' she told Darcy, and Darcy smiled at her.

'That's right. So Jamie will still need a paediatric check

every month or so, but the hands-on, day-to-day orders will come from you. As long as he agrees to obey them, we have a deal. We'll become a family.'

'And if I don't?' Jamie's chin tilted and Susie guessed there'd been run-ins already—this wasn't a child to submit to decrees with ease.

'I'm marrying Susie so we can get your health back,' Darcy said bluntly. 'That's a big thing. I won't do it unless you agree to follow medical orders. It's not worth it otherwise.'

'You mean you really don't want to marry Susie?'

'I don't want to marry anyone.'

Silence. Jamie thought about it for a little and then shook his head. 'I expect you do,' he said. 'Everyone does really. They just say they don't want to get married because they think it's sissy.'

Hmm. Susie watched Darcy's face. She was fascinated by what was going on here. The man looked confounded—almost as if he'd been caught out.

Sissy…

Nope, whatever else you could call Darcy Hayden, it wasn't sissy.

Darcy was knocked right off balance. Finally he took a deep breath and pulled himself together. 'Nevertheless, you'll follow orders, young Jamie.'

'What sort of orders?' Jamie eyed Susie with suspicion and Susie thought fast. What did Darcy expect here? It was some compliment he was paying her, she thought. Placing Jamie's health in her hands…

So turn into a doctor.

Jamie should be working toward a gradual return to health, she thought. Normality. That was mostly what was required. There were no magic cures for chronic fatigue syndrome. It was a disease that seemed to occur when the body's defence mechanisms had been put through too much, and patience and time and peacefulness seemed the only cure.

Normality. And normality meant for Jamie…a family.

A mother.

But how to put a mother's orders into the guise of a doctor's prescription?

'How long is it since you've been to school?' she asked curiously, and Jamie frowned and cast a suspicious look at his uncle.

'Answer Susie, Jamie,' Darcy said gently. 'She's the doctor here.'

Another dark look. Susie was obviously OK, but doctors weren't. He'd have had enough, Susie suspected. An overload of medical tests and diagnosis and treatments. 'Since I got pneumonia,' he said at last. 'About three months ago.'

'Hmm.' Susie looked at him assessingly, and her mind was in overdrive. 'Do you have school friends?'

'I did.' Jamie visibly shut off. 'I don't see them much any more.'

The child was growing increasingly isolated, Susie thought, and a glance at Darcy's face told her she was on the right track. The kids at school obviously liked him, though. Laura's reaction the night before had been defence of a friend.

So get those friends back…

'Well, as your doctor—'

He was still in anti-doctor mode. 'You don't look like a doctor.'

'I am.' She mock frowned at him and succeeded in drawing a reluctant grin. 'A fat one but a very stern one. As your doctor, I've decided we'll take a lunchtime constitutional together.'

'What's a consti…constitutional?'

'A brisk form of exercise,' she told him. 'Or actually not all that brisk. A sort of waddly form of exercise designed for pregnant mums and boys with CFS. What I figure is that every lunchtime we'll walk down to the school.'

'I can't walk.'

'There's the beauty of it,' she said gravely. 'You get to sit in the wheelchair and help push the wheels when I get tired, and I get to walk behind you and rest my tummy on your wheelchair handles. And every lunchtime we'll collect your school work for the day and say hi to your friends.'

'You mean go to school every day?'

'Just for a visit at first,' Susie said. 'You can stay for a while if you want, but—'

'I don't want.' His voice rose in panic and Susie nodded.

'No. That's fine. It's your decision when you go back. But we collect your school work, we say hi to your friends, we come home and you do a little bit of physiotherapy with me. I do a very nice back and leg rub. Then you do a couple of sessions of school work during the afternoon and next morning. Not for long. Say half an hour each. Then we take your work back to be corrected and collect the next lot.'

'And that's all?' Jamie was looking at her suspiciously.

'For the moment,' she said serenely. 'But I bet it'll help.'

'How will it help?'

Any medical treatment would be eyed with distrust, Susie thought, watching his face. He'd been through enough.

'It'll stop you falling behind with your school work so when this disease is cured—which it will be—you won't have to drop back a grade.'

He blinked. He clearly hadn't thought of dropping a grade. Susie could tell the very thought was appalling. 'I don't want to stay in grade four!' he said, stunned. 'I'm in grade five after Christmas.'

'Of course you are.' Susie approved. 'But when you get better—'

'I don't know if I will get better.'

'You will.' Susie rose and walked across to him, then stooped before his wheelchair and took both his hands in hers. Still Darcy had the sense to stay silent. 'Jamie, you have chronic fatigue syndrome. It's a disease that lots of people have had before you and lots of people will have again. And those people get better. You will get better, Jamie. It's just a matter of letting your body rest enough so it can recover at its own pace.'

He stared at her, his eyes enormous and full of mistrust. 'You promise?'

He must be so frightened, Susie thought, and wondered whether half the cause of his illness now was fear. To have his world crumbling around him, and then his body betraying him as well...

'I promise,' she told him. 'I swear.'

'When?'

'I'm not making promises on that one,' she told him. That'd be a stupid thing to do. 'Some people can take a long time to get better from CFS and some people get better very quickly. What I do think is that if you stay here, with Darcy and me and your grandma, you do the things we tell you to do and you stay in touch with your friends, then you won't get worse, and gradually we'll get you better.'

'You really mean it?'

'I really mean it.'

He stared at her for a long moment, and then he turned his chair so he faced Darcy head on. 'She's OK,' he said, and he was talking half to Darcy and half to himself.

Darcy grinned at his intentness. 'Yep. She's OK.'

'Can I go and tell Gran?'

'Before you do, Jamie, we need everyone to believe Susie and I met in England and decided to get married then,' Darcy told him urgently. 'Yesterday was so dreadful no one thought to gossip about Susie's return, but now they will. Can you help us here?'

He considered this with small-boy seriousness. 'You mean you want me to say you were all lovey-dovey from the start?' His face broke into a smile. 'Yuck.' But then his brow creased, still giving it serious thought. 'Yeah, I'll say it. But can I whisper the truth to Grandma? She'll help.'

'Of course you can.'

And suddenly everything was just fine with Jamie. 'Yes!' It was an exclamation of joy. He spun his wheelchair Grandma-wards. 'I'm going to see her right now,' he flung over his shoulder as he zoomed out of the room. 'And then I'm going to visit Laura in the kids' ward and tell her—and I'll make your romance sound so corny that even she'll believe it.'

Then Susie and Darcy were by themselves, and suddenly there was nothing to say.

The kettle started to boil. It whistled into the silence and then switched itself off. Still silence. What had they done?

'It seems we've organised a marriage,' Darcy said at last.

'We have.' She felt she was stepping on eggshells. 'What made you change your mind?'

'A sleepless night. The impossibility of any alternative.'

She looked doubtfully at his face. For her this seemed a reasonable option but for him... 'You know, you could put Jamie in foster-care and he'd probably survive,' she said slowly.

'I could do that.'

'So why don't you?' There weren't many men Susie could imagine doing what Darcy was doing—for a child who wasn't even his son. In fact, there wasn't one!

'I spent an incredibly lonely childhood,' he said softly. 'My mother and my sister didn't give a damn. The only thing that kept me sane was that my father loved me, and I can't bear for Jamie not even to have that.'

'So you'd come half a world and even marry a stranger for him to have that.'

He shrugged. 'It's no big deal.'

'I think it's a very big deal.'

She couldn't help herself. Darcy was sitting at the table and he was staring into space as if it didn't matter that he'd just committed himself to so much for one small boy. It was too much. Without thinking for one more second, Susie leaned over the table and she kissed him squarely on the lips. And something happened…

It was supposed to have been a kiss like the one he'd given her the night before—light and warm and caring. It was supposed to have been a kiss of appreciation.

But it was nothing of the kind.

In that moment when their lips met something changed. It was as if the air around them had suddenly received an electric charge. Susie's lips had intended to just lightly brush Darcy's, but instead…

Instead they locked onto his, as if they'd been charged with something she couldn't handle—magnet meeting metal and holding. There was some power here that she didn't understand in the least, but it held them tight against each other and wouldn't let them go.

It warmed them—it seared—from the toes up, and it locked their bodies together as if two beings were merging to become one.

It was a kiss, but it was so much more…

It was the beginning of something wonderful, Susie thought, and when it finally ended it had her sagging down into her chair and staring across the table in stunned amazement.

That wasn't meant to have happened. Neither of them had willed it.

But it had just been a kiss. Hadn't it?

No. Darcy was looking as blankly stunned as she felt, and she knew that he'd felt whatever it had been as strongly as she had. Wow!

She'd never felt like this with Charlie, she thought dazedly. Like she was being lifted from her own body and transformed into something else.

It must be her pregnancy, she thought desperately, searching for logic. It must be hormones or something. She dared another glance at Darcy and saw that he must be pregnant, too—or have the same hormones…

'Darcy, I didn't—'

And then another voice cut across the tension. 'Well, well, well. What do we have here?' They both spun like guilty teenagers and Robert was standing in the doorway.

It was such a relief! It was such a dissolution of tension that Susie almost laughed. But there was no laughter in Darcy's eyes. Instead, his face had become grim and intent, like his body had just betrayed him.

He stood, ignoring Susie completely and concentrating solely on the older doctor. It was as if every nerve in his body was concentrating on blocking the sensations of what had just happened.

It was Darcy who managed to speak first, and when he did his voice was as grim as someone announcing a funeral.

'I think you need to congratulate us, Robert,' he told the newcomer. 'You've just found yourself two partners instead of one—and you've just witnessed Susie's acceptance of my proposal of marriage.'

CHAPTER SIX

ROBERT thought the whole idea was fantastic—practical, workable and very, very funny.

'I told you she was a matchmaker,' he said, sitting down at the table and wiping his eyes. 'I went to bed last night feeling lousy as hell—partly because of what happened yesterday and partly because I'd put you in such a mess, boy. But I might have known our Susie would make it all right. It's fantastic!'

'It's not fantastic. It has major problems, but it'll serve the purpose,' Darcy retorted, still not looking at Susie.

'Yes, indeed.' The old doctor rubbed his hands together. 'It'll certainly serve the purpose. Whale Beach will have three doctors. Three!'

'Will we get away with it, do you think?' Susie asked doubtfully, and Robert smiled and smiled.

'Immigration won't question this, and I'd imagine the Medical Board will be delighted. This whole region has been a nightmare for them. With three doctors, Whale Beach will become a proper medical centre. We'll be able to expand. Instead of patients having to travel to other towns because I can't cope with everyone, we'll find patients travelling to us. It'll solve so many problems...'

'They'll ask why I applied for rural doctor status rather than stating that I was marrying,' Darcy pointed out.

'That's easy.' With such an enticement—two young doctors in the town—Robert was off and running in the invention stakes. 'You met early on when Susie went to England. I was worried about Jamie, I mentioned in my letters to Susie that Jamie had an uncle who worked near where she did, and she introduced herself so she could speak to you about my worries. Maybe you were at a medical conference together, and when she saw your name tag she stepped right up and introduced herself. That's probable. And it was love at first sight.' Robert beamed. 'Nothing could be more obvious.'

'But—'

'But, of course, Susie was married and then newly widowed.' Robert was allowing no interruption. He had it all sorted out in no time flat—and Susie was suddenly suspecting he'd thought of this marriage solution even before they'd thought of it themselves. 'So you were in love with Susie before you came out here to be with Jamie, but she was still getting over Charlie's death. She turned your proposal down. Then, after you left, she missed you so much—and you were living in the town she loved, and she was pregnant and alone...'

'Hey, this makes me sound pathetic,' Susie retorted, startled, and Robert grinned.

'That's right. A little pathos will go a long way in this touching tale. Now, if you can just make those big eyes fill with tears when you're talking to officialdom—and I know from past experience you can turn them on at will when you want something badly enough...'

'Robert. You're a—'

'A machiavellian schemer—just like you,' he told her approvingly. He beamed. 'Now, let's get this town's medical team organised.'

Which was why, by the end of the morning, Susie found her future mapped out and herself unpacking Darcy's precious condom boxes as well as the rest of his pharmaceutical supplies.

'Because until the baby comes we put you on light duties,' Robert had decreed. 'You're in charge of setting up the pharmacy.'

Darcy had said very little while Robert had planned, and Susie had simply been too stunned to argue. So now she sat surrounded by boxes of supplies and pharmacy paperwork, and she tried and tried to stop her head from spinning.

She was getting married!

Again.

The thought scared her to her socks, but then it became impossible to stop a frisson of excitement.

She'd enjoyed marriage. Because her mother had died early and she'd essentially been raised by her father and Robert, Susie was accustomed to male company. She didn't like living alone and marriage was the obvious solution. She'd met Charlie just as her father had died. Charlie had been a very good friend and their marriage had been built on trust and mutual respect.

And then there was sex…

Now, that was a problem. She frowned as she sorted tubes of cortisone creams into order. Sex…

With Charlie it had been lovely. They had been such good friends, and sex had been an extension of that friendship. Warm and comforting and safe.

It hadn't been exciting though, she remembered, and she'd always thought that somehow it could have been better. But he'd become ill so quickly that it had never happened. Still, even two years after Charlie's death, she ached for that aspect of married life, even if it never could be more exciting than she'd experienced already. The thought of spending the rest of her life celibate…

Whoa!

She sat back on her heels and blinked. What was she thinking here? This was a marriage of convenience, and the fact that she just had to look at Darcy Hayden and she was thinking about sex…

Well, she had to stop thinking about it, she told herself crossly. Concentrate on cortisone cream. Much more important than sex. If she got the percentages mixed up she'd have people losing skin all over the place, and Darcy and Robert would pack her off to England again so fast her feet wouldn't reach the ground.

Sex…

Darcy…

She sighed at the impossibility of separating the two—then looked up at the sound of approaching footsteps and there was Darcy looking straight down at her over the counter of their new little dispensary.

If he could read her thoughts… She blushed bright crimson, and as the colour swept all over her, she ducked her head and concentrated fiercely on percentages. One of the condoms she'd been packing was still lying on the floor. She stared down at it—and blushed some more.

Strangely, he didn't speak at once. She was aware of him watching her as she sorted tubes and blushed, but that was all he did. Watched.

'I'm getting it sorted,' she said at last, crossly. 'You don't need to check on me.'

'No.' He rounded the counter, knelt, lifted a pile of five-percenters and slotted them into their allocated place. 'I already have,' he told her.

'Checked on me?' Her eyes flew to his. They were a whole six inches apart and the heat in her face didn't abate one bit. 'W-What do you mean?'

'Last night, before I accepted your so kind proposal of marriage, I phoned the medical director of the hospital where you last worked.' His voice softened still further, making what he was saying weirdly intimate. 'His report was glowing. It seems we have us a fine doctor.'

Susie glared. 'But you had to check?'

'I had to check,' he said gravely. 'Of course. Maybe you should have, too. It's some commitment we're making.'

'Right.' Anger helped here, and her colour finally subsided. 'What about you, then? Are you a fine doctor?' But she knew. Unlike him, she hadn't felt the need to check, and the thought made her angrier still.

'Robert checked on me when I applied for a job.'

'I'm not Robert.' She glared, fuelling her temper. 'What sort of doctor are you? I mean, I know you can operate...'

'I'm a qualified surgeon,' he told her.

It didn't surprise her. The Caesarean he'd done had been perfect.

'But I thought you were in general practice.'

'I trained for surgery but I missed the people,' he told her. 'I liked being part of their lives. That's why I returned to general practice.'

'You like being part of their lives—because you don't want a life of your own?' It was a stab in the dark, but it hit a nerve. Darcy's face darkened.

'What do you mean by that?'

'Just that you don't want marriage. Or commitment.'

'What do you think I'm doing now?'

'Oh, you're marrying and committing,' she said. 'But not because you want to.' She was watching his face and she knew she was right. 'You're doing it because you think it's your bounden duty.'

He thought about that for a minute and then nodded. Agreeing. 'And you?' he asked as if her inquisition had given him the right to probe himself. 'You've been there before. So why did you marry your Charlie? I assume that wasn't duty.'

'Charlie and I were friends.' She managed a smile. 'He laughed at my jokes and I laughed at his.'

'And that's a good basis for a marriage?'

'The best,' she said firmly. 'So I married because I thought it might be fun. And...and it was.' For a bit. It was impossible to keep the note of sadness from creeping into her voice, and it was impossible for Darcy not to hear it.

'And it wasn't fun,' Darcy said, watching her face. He was still automatically sorting pharmacy supplies onto shelves. 'It was an appalling tragedy.'

'So that means your view's confirmed? Commitment leads to sadness?'

'For me it would.'

'That's your family history.' She nodded sagely. 'Yep, I can see that. Like varicose veins. Your mother had 'em, so therefore you will.'

'There's no reason to take this lightly.'

'No.' She managed a smile, and then struggled to her feet—no easy feat when one was almost eight months pregnant. Darcy hesitated for a fraction of a second—enough to let her know he was reluctant to make even this much contact after the kiss they'd experienced only hours ago. But finally he held out his hand and helped her to her feet.

And there it was again. The magnetism. The powerful warmth that almost melted them together and had Susie's colour mounting all over again. He was so...

Male!

She hadn't made love to a man for almost three long years, she thought suddenly, and now, desperately, she wanted to make love to this one. To Darcy. To her fiancé.

And pigs might fly before that happens, Susie told herself. What I need is a cold shower.

She couldn't have it. Instead she somehow had to block the feelings sweeping over her and get her face under control. 'Were you looking for me for something?' she managed. 'Other than to tell me my references are OK?'

'Yes.' He was still holding her hand, as if he didn't realise he was doing it, and it wasn't going to be Susie who pulled away. 'It's twelve o'clock. Lunchtime at school is in fifteen minutes. I phoned and told Jamie's teacher the plan, and I've just woken Jamie and told him we're ready to go.'

'We?' She blinked.

'For the first time I figured...' Yes, she thought with some satisfaction. He was right off balance, too. 'I figured we should go together. I mean, the aim is to present us as a family. Right?'

'Right.' She smiled at him and then looked down at their linked hands. 'Absolutely.'

He followed her gaze—and then hauled his hand back as if it burned.

'In public,' he said quickly, and her smile deepened.

'Of course. Where else?'

Medically the school trip was a huge therapeutic success, although Jamie was very, very nervous. In fact, if Darcy hadn't agreed to accompany them, Susie had the feeling she never would have got him there.

He hadn't been to school for months, and he'd cut himself off completely. Now he thought of himself as different—as an invalid—and the first contact would be the hardest.

But Susie knew she was right. She could still hear her old professor droning on and on.

'It's vitally important to treat chronic fatigue sufferers as if they have a condition that will get better. As soon as their carers start treating it as chronic—and the carer loses hope—you have an extra layer of depression to deal with and that depression may well be the thing that makes the syndrome last another year or more.'

So...

'This is just the beginning, Jamie,' she told him, walking beside him while Darcy pushed the wheelchair. 'You've reached rock bottom now. CFS doesn't get worse than this. What we need to do now is to slowly start the process of rehabilitation.'

Which started the minute they walked in the school gate. A cluster of children, just released from the classroom for lunch, saw them coming and crowded across to the gate to watch.

At first they stared in silence. Susie could feel Jamie cringe under their combined gaze, and she moved right into action. Bossy Susie at her best.

'OK, who's in grade five?' she asked, and a dozen hands shot up.

'Right, the rest of you clear off,' she told them. 'This is grade five business.' And all of a sudden it was. The grade-fivers, appealed to, reacted with authority and glared the rest of the onlookers away.

'Jamie's back,' Susie said to the remaining children. 'He's been dreadfully ill—as you can see—but he's on the way to recovery now.' Then she put on her helpless tone—the one that Darcy was starting to know. He cast her a suspicious look and she winked at him and turned back to the children. 'Now, who's Jamie's special friend?'

There was a fraction of a pause, and then half a dozen hands shot skyward. To be a friend to a kid in something as fascinating as a wheelchair seemed suddenly very desirable.

'Great,' Susie said. 'And I'd imagine the rest of you are his friends as well.' She gazed around her thoughtfully. 'You.' She pointed to the biggest boy with his hand up—a kid who had all the markings of the school tough guy about him. 'It's Tommy Guthrie, isn't it? It must be. You look just like your dad. Yikes, you've grown two feet since I last saw you.'

Tommy grinned. This obviously appealed, and he knew who Susie was. The whole town did by now. 'Yeah.' He lifted his arms and flexed his muscles. 'And I've grown crossways, too.'

'Are you strong enough to wheel Jamie in to meet his teacher? Miss Martin, isn't it?'

'Course.' His chest expanded a notch.

'You might need a couple of assistants to help you up the steps. Can you choose?'

'Mack and Fred,' Tommy said promptly, and Susie nodded.

'That's great.' She smiled around at the whole class of grade-fivers. 'And the rest of you... Can I trust you to make things easy for Jamie? Stop the other kids teasing him and stuff? Help with his wheelchair when he needs it?'

'Yeah.' The response was overwhelming.

And finally… 'Will you go with them now, Jamie?'

But Susie didn't need to ask. Tommy was already behind the wheelchair, Mack and Fred were at his side and Jamie was being reclaimed by his own. And his tentative smile said he thought maybe the idea was great.

'He's only allowed to stay for fifteen minutes,' Susie called as the procession moved importantly off. 'We'll wait here. Will you bring him back to us?'

'Too right,' Tommy said, and then was forced to pause as a small girl with red hair tugged Jamie's arm.

'If I stood on your wheelchair steps then they could push me, too.'

'We'll take turns,' another girl said, and Jamie disappeared, being pushed far faster than was safe, but in a welter of excited chatter and an overloaded wheelchair in the direction of Miss Martin.

'That,' Darcy said as the wheelchair rose precariously up the steps and disappeared into the building, 'was brilliant.'

'I'm a great organiser,' Susie said smugly. 'Robert told you that.'

'I can see.' He eyed her and there was a trace of doubt behind his smile. 'I'm beginning to wonder what on earth I'm letting myself in for.'

'A very organising wife,' she said serenely, and peeped a smile up at him. 'But don't worry. I won't organise you. Well, not very much.'

By the time they were due to be married, Darcy was starting to get a very clear idea of what Susie meant by 'not very much'.

It meant a lot.

She was simply the bossiest, most managing female he had ever set eyes on, he decided. They'd applied for a marriage

licence. There was a minimum waiting period of four weeks
and it took a little longer to make sure immigration and medical registration would be OK.

In those weeks Darcy had worked beside Susie as a doctor,
he'd acted the devoted fiancé during immigration interviews,
but as far as any other contact went he kept his distance.

Or he tried desperately to keep his distance. It was pretty
much impossible when they lived in the same house, they
practised medicine in the same hospital, they operated together, they discussed patients, they shared the same concern
for Jamie...

They even ate at the same table. They discussed medicine,
Jamie chattered about everything under the sun, but between
Susie and Darcy there lay restraint.

Or maybe that wasn't true. It was certainly restraint on
Darcy's side but it was consideration on Susie's. She knew
he was feeling the pressure.

He was acting like a caged tiger, Susie thought as she
watched the tension build, and she wondered more and more
whether, when the time came to marry, he really would go
through with it.

He had to. For Jamie's sake.

And medically he had to, for Whale Beach's sake.

In five short weeks the place had been transformed. The
practice was working like a dream, with Robert only doing
morning surgery, Darcy doing afternoons and Susie evenings.
Sometimes they overlapped, but no matter how busy they
were Robert was packed off at noon each day 'to paint, to
do the physiotherapy exercises you've been set or to rest'.
Susie herself had driven Robert to Hobart to be thoroughly
medically assessed and was bossing him into acquiescence.
'Or else!'

In consequence, Robert's health was improving by the day,
so much so that he was talking about doing more.

Their little pharmacy was running brilliantly. No longer
did patients have to wait for much-needed medicines. Even

the condom supply was decreasing, and medically the queues in the waiting rooms had disappeared. Already patients were coming from other towns where medical resources were stretched past their limits. Mothers were bringing their daughters from thirty miles away—'I'd be more comfortable with her seeing a lady doctor' or 'I've always hated the idea of having a man take a pap smear...'

Darcy and Susie were running two surgical sessions a week for planned operations, plus they were coping well with emergencies. Susie's anaesthetic training meshed beautifully with Darcy's surgical skills, and surgery cases which had previously been sent to Hobart were now being attended to in the town.

And Jamie was looking so much better. He was doing more and more, and his time spent sleeping was reducing by the day.

So there was no reason for Darcy to back out—was there?

He couldn't. They'd had to take on extra nurses and the town was buzzing about its wonderful new medical facilities.

As they were about the impending wedding.

'It's just so romantic.' Kerry Madden had come in for her first check-up since she'd been released from hospital in Hobart, and it was Susie she'd elected to see. 'Darcy's so nice,' she told her. 'You're so lucky to have waited.'

'You forget—I've been married before. I've hardly been pining on the shelf.' Susie was taking Kerry's blood pressure and giving an inward sigh of relief. The reading was close to normal. There seemed so few after-effects from her brush with death that Susie could hardly believe her luck. Medically Kerry seemed out of the woods.

Not psychologically, though. She'd lost her baby, the grief was still raw and dreadful, and she'd come near to death herself. It had been a life-changing experience, and now Susie sat back and surveyed her friend with concern. 'How are you coping?' she asked.

'What with?'

'With everything,' Susie said gently. 'With coming back to the farm. With the children and Steve. With the loss of your little one.'

For a moment she thought Kerry would say nothing—pretend things were OK. And then she took a deep breath and the floodgates opened.

'I'm not.' Kerry closed her eyes for a long moment, and then opened them and stared across the desk at Susie. 'I can't...I can't cope with Steve,' she admitted. 'He pretends nothing happened. He won't talk about our baby. You know we buried him as soon as I got back to Whale Beach. The undertakers had waited because I thought it was so important that I be here—but Steve wouldn't even come. He thought it was stupid. Forget it, he says, and he thinks I should get pregnant again straight away.'

'You mustn't do that,' Susie said urgently, startled into imperatives. 'You know that. Your body needs time to get over this battering.' She hesitated and then ploughed on. There was no easy way to say it, but it must be said. 'Kerry, you lost this baby from eclampsia. If you become pregnant again—especially straight away—then you risk exactly the same thing happening, and this time you might lose your own life as well as the baby's. You have five other children to consider. You mustn't.'

'I know.' Kerry gulped down a sob. 'The doctors in Hobart told me. But...Steve wants...'

'I would imagine that Steve wants you more than he wants another baby,' Susie said gently, and Kerry shook her head.

'N-no.'

'No?'

'He just wants a good time,' she blurted out. 'The farm where we live belongs to my parents and he keeps rubbing it in—that it's my farm. So he thinks I should do the work, despite the fact that the farm income supports all of us. It's an ongoing fight. My parents have their own place, but they won't deed the farm over to us because they don't trust Steve. And Steve hates it. But he won't take on any other job.

'Susie, I'm so tired, but I have to keep working because he keeps spending money. He gambles, he drinks far too much and he's at me and at me...' She took a deep breath and admitted her worst. 'He wants me for sex and nothing else.'

And there was only one thing to be said to that. 'Would you be happier without him?' Susie said gently, and Kerry flushed and stared across the desk at her. Her pale face lost even more of its colour, but then somehow her shoulders squared and she reached what Susie suspected was a conclusion that should have been reached a long time ago.

'Yes, I would,' she said at last, and her words were suddenly firm. And bitter. 'He's not faithful. And...and he hits me. I guess I've faced this all gradually over the years, only it's the first time I've ever admitted it to anyone else. He's nothing a husband should be. And I could cope on my own— I guess like you did when your husband died.' She looked at Susie, pleading with her with her eyes. 'I could cope— couldn't I?'

'I'll bet you could.'

'But...' Kerry faltered. 'How could I tell him?' She took a deep breath. 'If I ask him to leave...I daren't. He... When I say he hits me, I mean...he really hurts. He scares me— and the children.'

'So you'd like someone else to be with you when you tell him?'

'Yes.' There was no hesitation now. The decision had been made.

And there wasn't a social service department in this town, Susie thought reluctantly. Hmm. She looked down at her very pregnant self—she had three weeks to go—and thought she was hardly the person to cope with a man who could be violent.

'How about if we ask Darcy to be with you when you tell him?' she asked.

Kerry stared. 'You'll volunteer your husband? Won't he mind?'

That brought a grin. 'He's not my husband for another four days,' Susie said blithely. 'He's my medical partner, and I don't see why he shouldn't make himself useful.' Then, as Kerry gave a reluctant giggle, she raised her eyebrows and gestured at the intercom on her desk. She knew Darcy was in the next room. 'Shall I call him in to discuss it?'

Kerry took a deep breath, her laughter fading. Almost visibly she straightened her shoulders again. And came to a final decision. 'If I go home now, I'll be pregnant again in weeks,' she said. 'He thinks having kids makes him seem virile. If he catches me taking the Pill he'll bash me. So, yes, please. If Dr Hayden would…'

Dr Hayden would. Darcy came into the room at Susie's summons, he leaned against the wall and listened while Susie outlined the problem, and his face turned grim as she spoke.

He went straight to the nub of the matter. 'You say he hits you?'

'Yes.' Having gone so far, Kerry had passed the point where pride was keeping her silent. She turned her neck and pulled down her collar, and an ugly blue-green bruise was exposed for them to see. 'I'm still so tired.' She looked pleadingly at both of them as though she wasn't sure that they'd understand. 'The night before last I asked him if he'd milk the house cow, and then, when he said he wouldn't, Lisa— our eldest—told him he was lazy. So he hit Lisa, and then when I tried to stop him he hit me. It…it happens all the time. Mostly it's just me, but increasingly he's hitting Lisa and Sam, and the other kids will get it eventually.'

'And he hits hard.' Darcy fingered her bruise, tracing its edges. 'That's a nasty haematoma. Hell, Kerry. You could have him arrested for this.'

'That's not a bad one. He broke my arm once,' Kerry said diffidently. 'At least, I was sure it was broken but I wasn't game to come and see a doctor. Steve would have had a fit.

I just tied it up and kept going. And my fingers. He bends my hands back...'

'We'll take X-rays,' Darcy said firmly. 'Now. With evidence of old breaks, with that bruise on your neck and a signed statement by you, we'll get an on-the-spot intervention order to keep him away from the farm. We can contact Social Services in Devonport and they'll take it from there, organising access visits to the kids and so on, but that can wait. For now we get the police order, and then we'll break the news to Steve.'

'But...' Kerry faltered. 'Can I really ask him to leave?'

'The farm's in your parents' name, isn't it? I imagine your parents could ask you all to leave if they wished. Couldn't they?'

'Yes, but they wouldn't. They want the farm to be mine.'

'Would they support you in asking Steve to leave?'

That was obviously an easy question to answer. 'Yes. They hate him.'

'Then you're home and dry. And Steve's parents live close by,' Darcy told her. 'It's not as if he hasn't anywhere to go, and any number of people will testify that he's put nothing into your farm. He has no rights here apart from arranged access to his children.' He glanced again at her neck and his eyes darkened. There was no excuse for doing this to a woman. 'You're doing the right thing, Kerry.'

The weary woman looked at Darcy for a long minute. She looked at Susie and then back to Darcy.

'I need to do this,' she said at last.

'You do.'

'It just seems so...hopeless.' Her eyes blinked back tears. 'There's just nothing to look forward to any more. Nothing.'

'Yes, there is,' Susie said suddenly. She'd been thinking while Darcy had been doing his organising. What was needed here—seriously—was some light relief. 'What are you doing on Saturday?'

'Saturday?'

'It's our wedding day,' Susie confided. 'Darcy and I had thought we'd just pop down to Hobart and get married in a registry office—but if I can fix it in time, I've just changed my mind.'

'You've…' She had them both staring at her, but Susie wasn't to be stopped. She was in organisational mode again.

'What this town needs is a party,' she said. 'A proper wedding. And if we're having a proper wedding I need a matron of honour and a flower girl. Kerry, you were my best friend at school, and there's no one closer to me now. If I pay for the dresses, will you and Lisa do that for me?'

'Oh, Susie!' As a tonic it was amazing. Kerry even managed a smile. 'Really? And you want Lisa, too? She's been so miserable.'

'Of course I want Lisa.' Susie cast a sideways glance at Darcy to see how he was taking it, but he seemed too stunned to speak. Good. 'Jamie's being page-boy, and Robert will be Darcy's best man. We'll have a proper wedding ceremony in the little church on the headland, and then we'll organise a party to end all parties.'

'Hey, hang on a minute…' Darcy sounded stunned to the core but Susie fixed him with a look. She sent him a silent message and then she smiled again. This time at Darcy.

'Don't you think we need a party, darling?' she said sweetly. 'If I can arrange it?'

'I'll help,' Kerry said eagerly, and Susie looked at her and thought, Yes, this was the right thing to do. Some medicines didn't come in bottles. Sure, Kerry had enough to organise on her own behalf, but an offer of rekindling a friendship, and something to think about over the next few awful days— something to take the town's notice from her separation— was just what she needed.

And Darcy knew it. He couldn't refuse.

'OK,' he said finally. 'If you really want it.'

'I'm going to be the world's tubbiest bride,' Susie said cheerfully. 'But, yes—this is what I really want.'

CHAPTER SEVEN

IF THERE'S one thing small Australian towns were good at, it was organising celebrations, and on this occasion Whale Beach outdid itself.

Once the townsfolk learned what Susie wanted they came out in force. There'd been mutterings of disgust about the couple's intentions to marry in a Hobart registry office. Apparently the town thought this was just how things ought to happen, and they wouldn't be stopped by the lack of a bit of organisation. The fact that there were only three days left to organise was held to be no impediment at all.

'So we're having four hundred guests?' Darcy said incredulously, late on Friday afternoon.

He, Susie and their attendant nurse—Lorna Touldbridge—were painstakingly cleaning gravel from the elbows and forearms of Harry Blake. Harry, an enterprising eight-year-old with more courage than sense, had accepted a bet from his mates. He'd pushed his bike up to the top of Gandilong Bluff and had tried to ride to the bottom. It was a downhill distance of about half a mile by the gravel track—or about a hundred yards as the crow flew.

The crow might have flown but Henry couldn't, and neither had he been able to control his bike on such rough ground. The result was truly and bloodily spectacular. Luckily he'd been wearing thick cargo pants which had prevented major damage to his legs, and he'd thrown his arms up to protect his face. If he hadn't, they'd be transferring him to Hobart or even to the mainland for the attention of a plastic surgeon.

As it was, it was a job to be done under a general anaesthetic, and a couple of hours' intricate cleaning of every inch of exposed skin. Henry was going to be a very sore little boy for a long time. Darcy and Lorna cleaned as Susie kept careful watch of the child's breathing while she monitored the anaesthetic. The damage was too extensive to be done under a local anaesthetic, and the child was badly shocked, which made her job doubly tricky.

Still, there was time to talk, as there hardly had been since their decision to wed in public. Darcy had simply acquiesced. 'Anything to make Kerry's life more bearable,' he'd said, and little else, and he'd stayed as remote as he'd ever been.

But now...

'Four hundred guests?' Susie glanced up from her patient, her eyes widening as Darcy asked the question. She didn't know anything about four hundred guests. 'Where on earth did you get that number?'

'From me,' Lorna said in satisfaction. The middle-aged nurse was in her element—in fact, it seemed as if all of Whale Beach was enjoying this course of events very, very much. 'Last count was four hundred and fifteen. Kerry's mum told me this morning. She's taking the RSVPs.'

'But—'

'And if you knew how pleased Kerry's parents are with you, you wouldn't begrudge them the trouble,' Lorna said, casting an approving glance at the pair of them before she went back to tweezing embedded gravel from Henry's forefinger. 'Kerry got pregnant by Steve before she had enough sense to know he was rotten through and through, and her parents have been watching on the sidelines in increasing worry ever since.'

'She's lucky to have them,' Susie said, with a doubtful look at Darcy. Intent as he was on the job at hand, he was, it seemed, still taking the four hundred guest list on board.

'She is.' Lorna wasn't to be stopped. 'They moved in two minutes after the intervention order was served, and they've changed all the locks. They've employed a man to stay in the outbuildings at night—because they don't trust Steve an inch and he's so angry he's capable of anything. And now they're so delighted Kerry and Lisa are part of your wedding that they've taken it on themselves to move mountains. And they have everyone in Whale Beach right behind them.'

'It was just supposed to be a party on the beach,' Susie said weakly. 'With bring your own food...'

'Well, that wouldn't have been right,' Lorna said stoutly. She, too, took a peep at Darcy. She had the temerity to grin at the look of dismay on his face, and then she turned back to Susie. 'Kerry's mum is president of the local Country Women's Association. So they're catering.'

'But it'll cost a fortune!'

'Everyone who wants to come puts in,' Lorna said serenely. 'And so far I don't think there's a single occupant of this town who hasn't put in. Everyone wants to come.' Then she grimaced. 'Apart from Steve, that is, but we can ignore him. He deserves everything that he has coming to him, that one, and Kerry's mum told me this morning that Steve's own mum and dad have put their names down for the wedding. That's how much support he has.'

'It'll be hard for Steve to stay in Whale Beach under so much disapproval,' Darcy said, as if to thrust his mind from...how many? *Four hundred* guests?

'That's his lookout,' Lorna said stoutly. 'He's been knocking Kerry around for years and everyone knows it. Plus, he's got more than one girl into trouble—even after he was married. Because Kerry's put up with it the locals have kept it to themselves, but this wedding and you asking her to be your matron of honour—well, it's a celebration of more than just you two getting together.'

'I suppose so.' Darcy didn't sound the least bit sure.

'So you make sure you do us proud,' Lorna ordered. And then she looked sideways at the pair of them. Honestly, she thought. They looked so efficient and professional in their white coats but there were some areas where doctors were just hopeless. 'You know,' she ventured, 'Kerry discovered yesterday that Jamie didn't even have a dinner suit.'

'A dinner suit?' This time it was Susie who stared. 'Jamie?' Early in their relationship she'd taken the little boy shopping in Devonport. He now had a great new wardrobe, consisting mostly of surf gear which he'd decreed was cool, and she'd told him he could wear anything he liked to the wedding. He'd chosen a particularly garish surf shirt and cargo pants—like every other kid in the neighbourhood wore.

'He's a page-boy and he'll dress accordingly,' Lorna said sternly. 'Kerry's Lisa explained it to him—that it wouldn't be proper to wear anything else. Kerry's dad's driven to Devonport this morning to collect the hired suit. Oh, and the cake…'

'The cake?'

Both doctors were looking weak-kneed, and Lorna thought, Great. Kerry had asked her to let them know just how big this was going to be, so she'd chosen her time wisely to break the news, and they could hardly back out now.

There was little more to be said.

'Maybe we should concentrate on Harry,' she said blithely, going back to tweezing. 'Because he's on the guest list, too, and his mum's organised a wheelchair already.'

Which left them so organised there was nowhere for them to go but forward.

'It's going to be neat,' Jamie told them as Susie tucked him into bed that night. He was so much better now that her heart lightened every time she saw him. She and Darcy had worked as a team. There was almost always one of them with him, and when there wasn't he'd spend his time with his beloved gran.

There'd been no more infections. All it took now was confidence, Susie thought, and he'd be back on his feet. But for that confidence to build, there had to be security and love.

And Susie had so much love to give. She had it in buckets,

she thought, and she was aching to share. With her own wee one, with this little boy—and with his stubbornly unlovable uncle.

Susie had taken to coming into Jamie's bedroom after Darcy had said goodnight and giving the little boy a cuddle of her own. For the first couple of times he'd resisted, holding his thin frame rigid in her clasp, but now he snuggled into her just as if he liked it. Which, underneath his small-boy pride, he did. 'All my friends are coming,' he told her proudly.

'And you're wearing a dinner suit.' Susie smiled down at him and shook her head. 'I can't believe it.'

'Lisa said I had to.' He tried to sound disgusted but it didn't quite come off. 'But Lisa and Kerry said Uncle Darcy will be wearing one, too. He will be, won't he?' The child was suddenly anxious, and Susie frowned. She hadn't asked what Darcy intended wearing.

'I'm not sure,' she said tentatively. 'We'd better ask the man himself.' She rose and went out to the hall to call him, and then Darcy was in Jamie's room and the usual tension settled between the pair of them. It was as if he knew how much she wanted to broach the barricades—and he was intent on building them stronger.

OK. She wasn't doing any broaching now. She was just reassuring Jamie. 'Jamie wants to know if you're wearing a dinner suit like his,' she asked stiffly.

For a moment, Darcy didn't answer. He stood looking down at her as she settled again on the bed beside Jamie. They were quite a sight—his very pregnant intended bride and his pale little flannelette-clad nephew snuggled up beside her.

They were both looking at him with equal degrees of anxiety, and for the life of him he couldn't stop a smile. They looked so...

So right. He acknowledged it to himself, and as he did part of his tension slipped away. Susie had done Jamie nothing but good. She was sitting on his bed, the little boy was nestled into her side and he thought, I've given him a mother.

She'd made no promises about that, he thought, but it was clear all the same. Susie's body language was such that if anything threatened her little boy she'd have that threat for dinner—a mother dragon defending her own.

And Jamie was so different now. He was still confined to a wheelchair—it was almost as if it was a security blanket that he refused to release by practising walking on a frame—but he was so much more relaxed. He was putting on weight, and he was chattering and losing that hard-plated defence that held the world at bay.

There was more to medicine than medicine, Darcy thought, and his smile broadened. For Jamie, Susie was a tonic all on her own.

But they were both waiting for an answer. 'Does that smile mean you're planning on wearing jeans and an old T-shirt?' Susie said suspiciously, and he grinned.

'Kerry would kill me. Followed by Jamie. Nope. Kerry's given instructions all over the place, and I have mine. I'm wearing a penguin suit, ma'am, just like Jamie's. And what are you wearing, Dr Ellis?'

'That's for me to know and you to find out,' she said serenely. 'The only thing I can tell you is that it won't have a clinging waistline.'

'I can see that.' He looked down at her bulge and smiled again. 'You're getting very close. What if you go into labour tonight? That'd set the cat among the pigeons.'

'Pigs might fly,' she retorted. 'This baby knows its due date. That's in two weeks. Anyway, the way Kerry's organising things, she's probably organised a labour ward on the side. Just in case. Now, Jamie…'

'Mmm?' He was happy. Snuggled into his pillows, with Darcy and Susie laughing and relaxed, he looked for the first time since Susie had met him a child completely at peace with his world.

'You know what you have to do?'

'Lisa's told me,' he said. 'Lisa's got me organised.'

'We appear to be surrounded by a whole set of managing females,' Darcy told him, and stooped to kiss him lightly on the forehead. 'And, heaven help us, we can do nothing but what we're told.'

'We can't back out now.'

'No.' As Jamie slept, they'd walked silently out to the back verandah, each knowing almost instinctively what the other was thinking. This was a bigger production than either of them had ever envisaged.

'It's bigger than *Ben Hur*,' Darcy said slowly, and Susie looked uncertainly up at him in the moonlight and could only agree.

'Do you mind very much?''

'I can't mind,' he said heavily. 'It started out as a commitment to Jamie and now...'

'Now it's a commitment to the whole town,' Susie agreed. 'Scary, huh?'

'And what happens when Jamie's better, or when Muriel dies?'

'You'll want to pick him up and take him back to Scotland?'

'I could,' he said slowly, thinking the option through. 'He could adapt.'

'He's getting better by the day.'

'He is at that.' Darcy turned to her, and some of the tension faded. 'I have you to thank for that.'

'It's down to us both,' Susie told him. 'He's starting to be secure.'

'He has a mother and father and a grandmother.' The tension rolled back into Darcy's words. 'That's what he's feeling as if he has.'

'Mmm.'

'And if I take him away…' Darcy took a deep breath. 'No matter how cured he may seem, he may well revert.'

There was no doubting that. The doctor in her was forced to agree. As well as the part of her that was falling in love… 'I guess taking him back to Scotland would be a strain.'

'You know, this isn't looking like a temporary marriage,' Darcy said heavily.

'No.' Susie was no longer watching him. She'd turned and was looking out at the stars. 'It started out as an emergency marriage but long term…'

'Long term we may well be stuck with each other.' He sounded appalled and Susie winced.

'Jamie will grow up.'

'How long are we stuck together, then? Five years? Ten years? And the medical needs of the town won't have changed.'

Susie took a deep breath. 'OK,' she said softly. 'This is your last chance, but that chance is still available. Call the whole thing off and I'll walk away.'

'You'd do that?' His voice was impersonal and he, too, turned away—as if he needed to come to his decision without looking at her.

'I'd do that.' She bit her lip. It'd be dreadful—to dash so many hopes—but to trap a man into marriage… 'I'm not forcing you into this, Darcy,' she said firmly—more firmly than she felt. 'No matter how trapped you're feeling, I won't have you saying it's me doing the trapping.'

'But it is.'

'No.'

'It is. You see, I couldn't bear it if you walked away from here,' he told her, still with that strange, impersonal tone in his voice. 'I can't hurt you that much. You give and you give…'

This was crazy. 'You want *me* to call it off, then?' she said with asperity. 'Holy, heck! Darcy, to me this marriage seems a sensible solution. Not a deep, dark entrapment. It could also be fun.'

'Fun?'

'Yes.' Susie was infuriated with the man, and it helped. 'In case you hadn't noticed, this household isn't exactly lonely. We're making Jamie laugh. Jamie in turn is making us laugh, and together, medically and personally, we're achieving miracles. It's going to be a real pleasure watching Jamie improve and grow and become a loving, normal little boy. Oh, and by the way, I think we need a puppy.'

'A puppy?' Darcy said faintly, totally bemused, and Susie grinned.

'That's right. A puppy. Jamie needs something to be dependent on him. It's time he was out of that chair, and I think a puppy would help.'

'Oh, yeah?' he half jeered at her. 'And who'd exercise it and feed it and care for it?' She could see what he was thinking. More responsibility. It was coming at him from every direction.

She was still infuriated. 'We would,' Susie snapped. 'Jamie and me. This isn't more of your entrapment, Darcy Hayden. Puppies are great.' Then she softened a little, seeing the look of uncertainty wash across his face. 'You know, you could just enjoy it. I'm not like your mother or your sister. I'm here to stay. Now, if that makes you feel like running, then maybe you take after them—but *I* certainly don't. So...'

'So?'

'So you can get yourself married and become part of a family and enjoy it, or you can feel stuck for the rest of your life. Either way, once you've gone through with it I refuse to feel responsible. And that's all I'm going to say,' she retorted. 'Now, if you don't mind, I promised I'd drop in on Muriel before I go to bed—you know Lorna's offered to bring her to the ceremony tomorrow—and then I have a gentleman who needs catheterising. And—' she gave him a cheeky grin '—he asked specifically for me.'

'I can't imagine why,' Darcy retorted dryly, and Susie's twinkle deepened.

'Some people think I'm desirable,' she retorted. 'Just because you don't...'

He did.

That was the whole trouble, Darcy acknowledged to himself as he lay sleepless in bed later that night. Almost nine months pregnant, bossy and organising and always under his feet, Susie was starting to seem the most desirable woman he could imagine.

Why? How could he possibly be attracted to her?

It must be because he wasn't dating any other women, he decided. Back home in the UK, working in a major hospital in Edinburgh and then a smaller town within easy commuting distance of the city, he had rarely been without a partner. He'd moved on fast enough, but that had been no problem. Most of the women he'd dated he'd never had to see again.

But here, even before Susie had arrived, it had been difficult to be lightly attracted to a local woman. This was a tiny community. One date would have raised expectations he'd had no intention of fulfilling.

And now those expectations would be fulfilled tenfold. As of tomorrow he'd be married, and dating would be a thing of the past. He'd seen enough of the condemnation the community placed on Steve Madden to know that playing around wasn't an option.

Which left him permanently with Susie.

Who was gorgeous.

No!

It would be so easy, he thought, rolling over and thumping his pillow for the thirtieth time that night, to allow himself to be seduced by the prospect of family. Of love...

But love didn't last. It was a fantasy that destroyed people's lives. His mother and his sister had hurt Darcy beyond endurance. He'd watched his father break his heart, and he'd learned that loving meant exposure to unendurable pain.

Susie herself must know it, he acknowledged, otherwise this marriage would be impossible. She'd buried a husband, and she'd not be likely to expose herself to that sort of anguish again. So the arrangement must be formal. Unsentimental and non-sexual. A business arrangement only.

An emergency wedding that might well need to last for ever.

The problem with two doctors marrying, and the town's third doctor acting as best man, was that it left no room for emergencies. The wedding was timed for eleven. At ten-thirty a carload of kids rolled down the bluff a mile out of town and ended up in Casualty, with a combination of minor and not-so-minor injuries between them.

Which meant there was nothing for it but for the town's three doctors—plus Ian Lars, the doctor from Stony Point who'd decided this ceremony was worth celebrating—to take off their wedding finery, pin a notice to the church door and reschedule everything for three in the afternoon.

The wedding guests took it in their stride. These were local kids after all, and they were related or known to all. The Country Women's Association rescheduled their wedding lunch and called it wedding dinner, hot beef and turkey became cold collation, Kerry took Jamie and Lisa to the beach—'because they're bursting with excitement and Jamie'll make himself sick if he isn't kept occupied'—and the doctors got on with what they had to do.

Which, as far as Susie was concerned, wasn't much. The kids, in combination, had been extraordinarily lucky. She gave the anaesthetic for the repair of a punctured lung—which took an hour and was less complicated than they'd feared—she stitched one set of lacerations, but then she was put firmly out of the surgery by Robert, Ian and Darcy.

'You'll be fast asleep by the time you're married if you don't go and have a snooze,' Robert told her, in a voice that was sounding more and more like the confident Dr Robert of old. 'You're almost at term, my dear. Look after yourself.'

And with Darcy backing him up, and Ian sighing and saying he might have known this would happen but he'd take charge of the recovering teenagers while the actual ceremony was performed, there was little else she could do. So she retired to the bedroom she'd slept in as a child. She attempted to rest and failed, and then she sat and stared out the window.

And tried to think of Charlie.

His photograph was on her bedside table. She lifted it onto her knees and then sat and looked at it for a very long time.

She was doing this for him, she told herself. It was Charlie who had so desperately wanted this baby, and in marrying Darcy she was keeping Charlie's little one safe. So there was no way this marriage could be seen as a betrayal of her first love.

She was marrying for the sake of Charlie's child.

So why did it seem as if it was for herself?

A marriage of convenience couldn't work, she told herself, and the knowledge seared into her mind and stayed. They were kidding themselves. No contract to live in the same house for years—to share parenting as well as working side by side as doctors—could ever last the distance. Something would have to give.

There was a light knock and Kerry entered. She was dressed in a soft peach, strapless dress and she looked lovely. After her horrors of the last few weeks she looked almost serene and Susie thought that, at least for Kerry, this wedding arrangement was brilliant.

But how about for the bride and groom?

'It's time to dress again,' Kerry told her. 'The other doctors told me they'd sent you to rest, and I figured that was stupid. How could you rest? I thought you might be getting really nervous by now.'

'I am at that.' Susie gave the photograph a last glance and Kerry followed her glance.

'Is that your last husband?'

Your last husband. It sounded so…final. She flinched and Kerry saw it.

'I'm sorry,' she said softly. 'You must have loved him very much.'

'Yes.' Susie stared down at the laughing face of someone she hardly knew any more. They'd had so little time together before illness had struck…

Had she loved Charlie? It had faded so far into the past now that she couldn't tell. They'd been friends and then she'd nursed him to the end and promised to bear his child…

'What are you thinking?' Kerry asked quietly, watching Susie's face, and she saw her friend's mouth tighten in pain.

'I'm thinking.' She took a deep breath. 'I'm thinking it's time I put Charlie away,' she said. 'I loved him once, and part of me…part of who I am now is because of Charlie. But he wouldn't want me to spend the rest of my life in mourning. In fact, he'd be the first one to tell me to make the most of the rest of my life.' She took a deep breath. 'And to love again.'

And that was that. Carefully she opened her bedside drawer and placed the frame carefully away. Life was for now. Life was for moving on.

Life was…Darcy.

'I'm not going to waste a second of this marriage,' she said softly. 'I feel like I've been given another chance.'

'Because you love Darcy?'

Soon she'd be formally asked that question, Susie thought. Soon she'd be standing in front of every person in Whale Beach and they'd be waiting for her response.

And she thought of Darcy. Darcy as she'd last seen him, his medical coat stained, and his eyes filled with concern. He'd been taking a hysterical teenager's hands into his and holding her tight as she'd lain on the stretcher.

'No one's been killed,' he'd said in a voice that had resonated with reassurance. It had sounded throughout casualty, reaching the other injured kids and giving them the same message. 'You've just given yourselves a hell of a fright but there's no permanent damage. You, Helen, have broken your leg, which means you'll be wearing a cast for a few weeks, but that's no cause for hysterics. You've all been very, very lucky. Now, I have a wedding to attend, as I'm sure you all know, so let's cut the histrionics and get on with treating you.'

Let's get on...

Darcy gave himself to everyone, Susie thought. He'd given up his job, his country—everything—to keep Jamie safe. He'd even agreed to marry her!

How could she not love a man like that? Even if he was incapable of loving her back.

'Yes,' she said at last to Kerry's still unanswered question, and she knew she was right. 'I love him very much.' She closed her bedside drawer with a final snap, placing Charlie's memories firmly where they belonged. In the past.

Those memories wouldn't stop her putting everything she had into this marriage, she thought, and if that meant laying her pride on the line and loving Darcy to bits, even if it was unreturned, then that's just what she'd do.

This might be an emergency wedding—but Susie was playing for keeps.

And finally she was there.

She wasn't everyone's ideal bride, Darcy thought in wonder as he watched her pause at the far end of the aisle. Her pregnancy was almost full term; there was no way of disguising it, and she hadn't even tried.

She'd driven to Hobart to choose her dress—'something pretty, but sensible and practical that I can take in afterwards'—but at the last minute practicality had deserted her. The shop assistant had asked what the dress was for, and when she'd been told she'd gone all misty-eyed.

'Oh, but you can't be practical. Not at a time like this. And look what we have!'

Susie had looked—and was hooked.

The dress was almost white, but the gorgeous shot silk was shadowed with soft apricot, the colour appearing and disappearing as the dress swirled in lovely folds around her. It had tiny shoestring shoulder-straps and a sweetheart neckline, and it was gathered under her breasts and then allowed to fall in luxurious swirling folds down to the floor.

It was meant to be her dress, the shop assistant had declared, and now, as he watched Susie walk steadily along the aisle toward him, Darcy could only agree. She looked fair and vulnerable and lovely. The wispy trailing bouquet of white roses and baby's breath and the single row of her mother's pearls around her neck were her only ornaments.

She wore no veil. Her curls fell softly onto her bare shoulders. Her eyes were calm and serene, and she walked toward him with a tiny smile on her lips.

She looked almost as if she loved him and it was enough to take a man's breath away.

Dimly Darcy was aware of Jamie wheeling himself before her, the ring resting on a satin pillow on his knees. And Kerry and Lisa were her attendants, smiling broadly enough to take away their own heartache.

He was aware of them—but mostly he was aware of Susie.

What had he thought she'd look like? he wondered. Whatever it had been, it wasn't this. This embodiment of womanhood. This vision of serene and utter loveliness was…his bride?

She was looking up at him and smiling, waiting for him to respond. The whole church was waiting for him to respond.

And finally he managed. Susie reached his side, she handed her bouquet to Kerry and then she tucked her hand into his.

'With this ring I thee wed...' The words floated into his head before the vicar had a chance to open his mouth.

He was about to say the words he'd vowed never to say, he thought dazedly, and when he'd made this decision he'd thought he could do it and stay heart-whole and fancy-free.

But she was so lovely, and she was looking up at him with just the faintest trace of anxiety in her gorgeous green eyes.

She was doing this for him, he thought. She could have forced him to leave town. She hadn't wanted to wed again.

Susie, the brave heart...

She was still smiling—and she was waiting.

And so, at last, he smiled, and she smiled right back at him. Trust me, her smile said. I'm trusting you. I'm placing my future in your hands, to do with as you will.

As he was. They were in uncharted territory here, but there was nothing for them now but to go forward. The whole community was waiting.

'Shall we get married, then?' he whispered, and her eyes lit up with relief.

'I think we should,' she murmured. 'Now that we've come this far.' She twinkled up at him, and for the life of him he couldn't help but respond. He chuckled, and the hand holding hers tightened and held.

And then there was nothing else to do.

They turned to the vicar and were made one.

CHAPTER EIGHT

THE party afterwards would be talked of locally for years. It went on and on into the night, the entire town assembling on the beach. The local band struck up and seemed ready to play until dawn, the food was so abundant there'd be left-overs to fill Whale Beach households for weeks, and the night was moonlit and perfect.

And Darcy and Susie hardly saw each other. Once the dancing began, the bride and groom were parted as they were partnered in turn by every avid dancer in the district.

Susie was whirled from one set of male arms to another. The locals loved her, and they were desperately happy at this solution to the town's needs. She was congratulated over and over, her eyes danced with the music and she hugged every-one in turn and thanked them for providing this party to end all parties.

It was wonderful, but it couldn't last for ever. It was Darcy who realised how she was feeling, and came to his bride's assistance. He simply removed the local lad who was cur-rently holding her, took her hand in his and turned and sig-nalled to the band to hush.

'My wife...' There was a general roar of approval at that, but he kept on. 'My wife, as you may have noticed, is just a little bit pregnant.' Laughter. 'And Jamie is weary, too.' He smiled across at the little boy and his smile said that Jamie was with them. One of them. Part of this new, won-derful family. 'So we'd like to thank you all for doing this for us—for giving us this celebration—and I hope you'll keep the celebrations up through the night on our behalf, but now it's time for us to go home.'

'But I'm not coming with you.' It was Jamie. He'd been

sitting on the sidelines, but his mates had been with him for most of the night, taking turns to shove his wheelchair along the sand wherever he wanted to go. And, as ten-year-old boys would die rather than dance, there'd been no problem with him feeling left out.

And now he sounded definite—yet content.

'You're not?' Darcy frowned. He was still holding Susie's hand, and his touch made her feel secure and very, very blessed. If only it was for real...

'Kerry says I should stay with her for two nights,' Jamie was saying. His eyes danced. For a child with CFS he was holding up extraordinarily well. 'Kerry says you need to have a honeymoon, and people have honeymoons all by themselves. And she also says kids think honeymoons are really, really boring. People just stay in bed all day.'

Susie blinked—and then blushed to the roots of her curls as the townsfolk laughed around her.

'Yeah, you get off on your honeymoon, the pair of you. If you don't get on with it soon, there'll be a baby in bed beside you,' someone called, and the crowd burst into even more approving laughter.

Then Kerry burst in. 'It's OK, isn't it? Taking Jamie home with me? Mum and Dad have said they'll stay with me and help.' Their matron of honour was trying not to laugh, but she was anxious. Very anxious. Had she done the right thing?

And standing in the moonlight, holding his new wife's hand, Darcy couldn't bring himself to say they didn't need—didn't want—a honeymoon. The whole town had arranged this—had wanted this—and, besides, if immigration officials were to be placated, they'd have to see a marriage.

'Of course it's OK. Thank you very much,' he said gravely. 'If it's OK with you, Jamie.'

'It's OK,' Jamie said smugly. 'Kerry says that it's what I have to do to have a family.' But then he frowned. 'Though I don't know what you'll do without me. Bed sounds boring.'

And as the locals laughed again, Susie stooped and kissed

him soundly. 'We'll miss you, that's what we'll do,' she told him.

'Yeah, but I'll be back Monday,' he said. 'And then none of us will have to go away again. Ever.'

Susie cast an uncertain glance at her new husband, and his face was inscrutable.

'No,' she said. 'We won't.'

'That's all right, then.'

But it was only weeks since Kerry had lost the baby and Susie looked doubtfully at her matron of honour. 'Kerry, you're exhausted. You shouldn't be taking on more.'

But even that had been arranged. 'I told you, my mum and dad are coming to stay to help,' Kerry said smugly. 'See? This town has it all fixed.'

'And all we can do is to go along with it.'

'I suppose so.' It was later still and they were being driven home. Kerry had taken the children home to bed, but the bride and groom had been held up for an hour more while the wedding guests had organised the traditional send-off. They'd formed a ring and had sung chorus upon chorus of 'Auld Lang Syne' while each guest said goodbye. As if they were leaving!

It was nonsense, but still it was traditional, and the locals would have it no other way.

Now their bridal transport—the local newsagent driving his precious model-T Ford bedecked with bridal ribbons and trailing a clatter of tin cans—was taking them back to their house. Alone in the back seat, there was so little and so much that had to be said.

'I'm not all that happy about Jamie,' Darcy said quietly, staring straight ahead into the night. As if he didn't wish to look at his new bride.

OK, Susie decided carefully. If he wanted to talk about Jamie rather than the wedding, she'd go along with it. 'Why not?'

'It's too soon for him to be staying away.' Darcy frowned. 'You didn't see him at his worst, but he's come so far. I don't want a relapse.'

'He wants to go.'

'I know. We couldn't refuse. As you say, all we can do is go along with it and hope it's not a disaster.'

A disaster...

Was he talking about Jamie or their wedding? Susie looked at his closed face, and she knew with absolute certainty that he was talking of both.

And then they were home.

At least the ceremony was over, Darcy thought. That had to be the worst. He walked up the verandah steps, then frowned as Susie gripped the rail. Hell. She really was exhausted.

'Getting married two weeks before a baby's due is hardly what I'd recommend as your doctor,' he said, and she managed an uncertain smile.

'You're my husband now—not my doctor,' she retorted. 'Robert says I'm fine, and so I am.'

'You're not. You're totally done in.'

'I'm OK. Honestly.' But there was just enough dogged determination in her voice to make him know better. He knew exhaustion when he heard it, and he heard it now.

He might not be her doctor—but he *was* her husband.

Right, then. There was a marital precedent for what he was about to do, if not a medical one. What was a man—a husband—to do?

What was expected, of course! So with one easy movement he swept her into his arms and cradled her against his chest, her lovely bridal gown streaming out behind. Lying in his arms, she felt soft and yielding and very, very lovely, and his gut kicked in recognition of...

Of what?

Of something he had to ignore!

Susie gasped in his hold, but he managed to ignore that,

too. Striding forward, he kicked the door open and carried his bride inside.

'Put…put me down.' It was all she could think of to say, and then, as he placed her on her feet and her heart thumped back into place, she gazed around their home and received another shock. The tension faded as surprise took over. 'What the…?'

What, indeed?

To mark their wedding, the community had moved mountains. During the ceremony and afterwards, while the bridal couple had danced obliviously on the beach, people must have slipped away. They must have done it in shifts, Susie thought dazedly, otherwise their absence would have been noticed.

'I don't believe this,' she whispered. The kitchen was festooned with white helium balloons—hundreds of them floating every which way. And the walls…

They'd been…painted?

The paint was hardly dry. The colour scheme hadn't been changed, but everything was clean and lovely. Dull drapes, stained from years of neglect, had now been replaced with new. The wooden table had been scrubbed and polished until it shone, as had the Baltic pine floorboards, and there were gay new cushions tied onto every chair.

Susie and her new husband could only stare. The smell of new paint and beeswax had their senses reeling.

A card stood on the table. It was large and white—the size of a glossy magazine—and it had a single golden wedding band embossed on the cover. Nothing else.

Stunned, Darcy lifted it, flipped it open and read it aloud.

'"You've given Whale Beach a medical team fit for a city,"' he read. '"In return, Whale Beach gives you a home fit for a marriage. Bless you both."'

And there were signatures. Looking over her new husband's shoulder, Susie saw that there was a signature from almost every inhabitant of Whale Beach.

'It's the town's wedding gift,' Susie whispered, gazing around the kitchen in awe. 'Oh, Darcy, it's lovely.'

But Darcy's face was more than bemused.

'A home,' he repeated. 'Not a kitchen. The card says a *home*. Shall we see what they've done everywhere else?' And without waiting for his bride to follow, he strode out to inspect the other rooms.

They, too, had been changed. 'Good grief.' Darcy reached the door of the sitting room and stopped dead.

'They must have planned this from the day we announced we were getting married,' Susie said, awed, as she looked at the gorgeous hand-sewn cushions in their newly painted sitting room. 'And how they did it…'

'They had just twelve hours.' Darcy was moving again. He hauled open Jamie's bedroom door and sighed with relief. It had been repainted, but essentially unchanged. 'At least they've had the sense to leave the bedrooms be.'

'N-no, they haven't.' While Darcy had checked Jamie's room, Susie had checked her own. She was standing in her bedroom doorway. Or what had been her bedroom.

The local women had had a field day here. Susie's bed was gone. Everything she knew was gone. The room had been painted out in a soft pastel yellow. New yellow curtains hung from the windows, emblazoned with tiny white teddy bears. In the centre of the room was the focus—the most gorgeous crib Susie had ever seen. The ceiling was hung with mobiles. There were piles of baby clothes on a new set of shelves.

It was just lovely. But…

'But where do they think I'm going to sleep?' Susie muttered, and she felt herself flush all over. Help!

'They've heaved all your stuff into the spare room. Everything.' After one swift look at the nursery, Darcy had gone on to find the spare room packed with so much stuff they couldn't make it all out. His amazement was fast being replaced by anger. 'Did you know about this?'

'No!'

He was hardly listening. 'It's stupid. As if they expect us to sleep together.' He was striding toward his bedroom—her parents' old room—and his voice was full of anger. 'Even if we wanted to, the bed's only comfortable if you sleep right in the middle. I don't know how your parents—'

And then he threw the bedroom door wide and his words were cut short.

'Oh...'

Susie, coming up behind him, saw what he saw.

And it was all just too much. She couldn't be angry in the face of a gesture like this, and her sense of the ridiculous surfaced to overwhelm her.

Her parents' ancient bed had disappeared. Instead, there was a bed to bedazzle. It was king-sized. It was made up with gorgeous red satin sheets—emblazed with hearts, for heaven's sake! And it had mounds and mounds of heart-shaped pillows scattered all over it. A soft white quilt was folded at the base of the bed—as if anyone could really want to sleep in a bed like this—and it, too, was embossed with silken hearts. And above their heads floated more helium balloons, this time red and white, all heart-shaped and painted with tiny Cupids pointing arrows straight down at the bed.

Susie choked back laughter but it bubbled to the surface regardless. It was too much. The thought of her friends sneaking away in relays while they were being married— heaving furniture, painting like madmen, carting cushion upon dazzling cushion...

'You *did* know!' Darcy's face was rigid, and his words were an accusation. He was feeling like he'd been placed in a trap and the sides were edging in on him. He stared down at the bed, and the thought of Susie in it...

The knowledge slammed home like a bullet. He wanted her!

No! His only reaction had to be anger. It was his only defence. 'You knew they were doing this!'

'I swear I didn't.' But it was hard for her to get the words out. Despite Darcy's fury, she couldn't stop herself. Choking with laughter, she sank onto the amazing bed.

And that made everything worse. The bed was armed. Susie hadn't noticed it, but there'd been rice paper carefully stretched across the ceiling. A fine thread had been attached to the mattress, and Susie's weight was enough to drag it down. The thread snapped, whatever was holding up the rice paper was no longer doing its job and it fell.

Releasing what it held in place.

A shower of confetti floated down over them both. It wisped down over Susie, laughing helplessly on the sumptuous bed, and on Darcy, who was standing stunned and furious beside her.

'Of all the…'

He was almost beyond anger. She was so beautiful and he wanted her so much—and he hadn't planned any of this! His nicely controlled world was spinning out of control.

He'd sworn never to become emotionally involved. Sure, he'd done the right thing by Jamie, but he hadn't expected to find himself loving the kid. And now he'd organised a sensible marriage and his wife had turned out to be a fruitcake.

An incredibly desirable fruitcake!

On the bed, Susie stared helplessly up at him, and put her hands out in a gesture of entreaty. She was trying hopelessly to stop laughing.

'Oh, Darcy, we might have known they'd do something.'

'Might we?'

Her laughter faded into uncertainty. 'Darcy, we're the local doctors. We're important to the community. They had to have some input…'

'Into our lives?' He looked around the room in disgust and her laughter died completely. He had to get out of there.

Away from her! 'OK, if you think it's funny, you sleep here. I'll do a fast check to make sure there's no problems in the hospital and tell Ian he can go home. Then I'll organise some bedding in the living room.'

But Susie sobered at that. His anger was enough to sober anyone. 'Then we'll have to fix the spare room,' she told him, calmer now. 'There's no way I'm sleeping in this crazy bedroom by myself.'

By myself...

It had been the wrong thing to say. The wrong thing to infer. As soon as the words were out she regretted them with all her heart.

'We're not sleeping together!' Darcy's words were snapping and hard.

She flushed to the roots of her hair. 'I wasn't inferring that we should.'

'I don't know what you were inferring,' he said wearily, raking his fingers through his thatch of dark hair. 'I'm too tired to think, but this is all nonsense. For tonight, though... Look, get some sleep and then—'

But he didn't finish his sentence. There was an urgent peal from the front doorbell, followed by a series of frantic knocks. Whoever was out there wanted them in a hurry, and there was only one reason for that. Honeymoon or not, this was the doctor's residence.

And Darcy switched into doctor mode just like that. Susie barely had time to get to her feet before Darcy had reached the front door. She entered the hall in time to see him fling it wide.

Kerry was there, and she was carrying Jamie.

Jamie was in trouble. The child was choking and gasping, his face was streaming with sweat and tears, and he was breathing way too fast. As Susie reached them, Darcy was already lifting the child from Kerry's arms. Exhausted, Kerry sagged to her knees.

'He...he just started choking,' she managed as Susie

stooped over her. She had barely enough strength left to whisper, 'No. Don't worry about me. Jamie…'

But Susie was checking Kerry first. There were two patients here and Kerry looked dreadful.

'I'd just put them to bed,' Kerry managed. 'Dad's gone back to their place and Mum's staying the night with me—to help. I left Jamie in the room next to me and I heard him. He said his chest hurt and he couldn't breathe. I was so scared. I just lifted him up and ran to the car…'

'Put your head between your knees.' Bride or not, like Darcy, Susie was right back in doctor mode. Heavens, carrying a ten-year-old so soon after what Kerry had been through was the worst thing Susie could think of.

'I'm…I'm fine.' Kerry was pleading. 'Look after Jamie.'

Only now did Susie flash a look at Jamie. Triage, drilled into every doctor at medical school, taught her to prioritise—if there were multiple casualties and multiple doctors then each doctor should check on individual patients. Only turn your attention to another after ensuring the condition you're checking is non-life-threatening.

And that's what Susie needed to do here. Even though Kerry clearly thought of Jamie as the patient, she was ill herself.

But now, satisfied that Kerry was recovering her breath and not about to pass out, Susie turned to see what was wrong with Jamie. Darcy had laid him on the floor and was ripping his shirt open at the collar. The child was frantically fighting for air and his eyed were terrified.

'I'll get oxygen.' Susie rose to fetch it, but Darcy shook his head. His fingers were holding the little boy's wrist, and the fear that had suffused his face when he'd first opened the door had eased.

'No. I think a paper bag.'

Susie's eyes flew to Darcy's face—and then back to Jamie. A paper bag.

Hyperventilation, then?

It made sense, she thought swiftly. Hyperventilation was mostly caused by a panic attack. Staying in a strange house might well have caused it.

Damn, they never should have agreed to it, she thought bleakly, but at least he'd be OK. This would cause no long-term damage. They just needed to calm him down, and breathing into a paper bag was the best way to force his breathing to slow. She flew through to the kitchen and grabbed what she needed, and by the time she arrived back, Darcy had Jamie in his arms and was holding hard. Reassurance was the first priority.

'Jamie, you're just having a panic attack,' he told him firmly. 'That's all this is. The excitement of the wedding and staying away from home has made your breathing speed up. So that's all that's wrong. I promise. It's called hyperventilation and it's not dangerous. The fast breathing makes your chest hurt. You must slow it down.'

He signalled Susie with his eyes as she stooped before him. 'Susie's here. She's putting a paper bag against your mouth and I want you to breathe into it. Slowly. I want you to breathe so the bag blows up and deflates again.'

His grip tightened on his nephew's shoulders. 'I know you can hear me, Jamie.' It was a stern order, harsh enough to make Susie blink. 'So do it. Now. Breathe. Wait. Then breathe again.'

Jamie's eyes flew wildly to his uncle's as Susie held the bag against his lips. There was nothing for her to do but reiterate his uncle's orders.

'Do it, Jamie,' she said.

'Your chest will stop hurting as soon as you slow your breathing,' Darcy told him strongly. 'Come on, Jamie. Breathe. Wait. Breathe…'

And slowly, slowly, the awful choking subsided and the little boy's rigid frame relaxed. The paper bag held against his mouth expanded and contracted, expanded and contracted, and it slowed with each breath.

Susie let her own breath out with a sigh of relief.

They'd been stupid to think it'd be OK for Jamie to stay with Kerry, she thought bitterly. But Jamie had wanted to so much. Kerry's parents had promised they'd stay to help, and he'd seemed so much better...

'He's OK,' Darcy said into the stillness. 'Jamie, you're fine.'

Susie glanced again at Kerry. The girl was shocked to the core. Wordlessly, she took herself through to the surgery, grabbed her doctor's bag and headed back.

Things might be improving for Jamie, but the priorities had changed again. She knelt beside Kerry and took the blood-pressure cuff from her bag. Darcy intervened.

'Let me.' His concern sounded in his voice, and it wasn't concern for Kerry or Jamie. He was prioritising, too. Hell, Susie was exhausted herself. She glanced up at him, and before she could protest he'd handed Jamie into her arms.

'Sit down and take him and let me see to Kerry,' he said. 'Jamie, you don't mind being cuddled by Susie, do you?'

Of course he didn't.

And Susie didn't mind herself. She sat down against the wall and gathered the little boy into her arms, and it was all she could do not to burst into tears over his head.

She'd only known this child for such a short time, and he'd wrapped himself around her heart like a hairy worm. He and his uncle both.

But at least she could cuddle Jamie.

'Oh, Jamie, you scared us silly.'

He'd scared himself silly. She could see that in his eyes, and in the way his fragile body trembled in her arms.

'Did you hear your uncle tell you what's happened to you? It's called hyperventilation,' she told him. 'It's quite common and it doesn't do any damage. It was just too much excitement so soon after being ill.'

It probably hadn't been the excitement, she thought. It would have been a proper panic attack—being left in a dark room in a strange house, and having no secure base.

He had a secure base now, though, she thought, and as the thought hit her, her own doubts faded. However much Darcy hated it, for now and for ever, they'd provided him with a family. And that family would exist even if it meant Darcy sleeping in the red satin sheets, she decided. He'd do it if she had to knock him out to get him there.

Meanwhile, Darcy, unaware of his wife's resolutions, was examining a protesting Kerry.

'Your blood pressure's sky-high,' he growled. 'For heaven's sake, woman, what were you doing, carrying him?'

'I thought he'd die.'

'We left him with you because your mum and dad promised to stay as well.' Darcy was clearly puzzled. 'Your dad's strong enough to lift him. Why didn't he bring him here?'

'Dad had to go home.'

'Why?' There were things going on here that Darcy didn't understand. Kerry's white face still reflected fear, but she could see for herself now that Jamie was fine. So what else was wrong?

'Steve,' she whispered.

'Steve?'

'He phoned just after we'd brought the children home from the wedding,' she said. 'And he said such things. He threatened me, physically threatened, but I said Mum and Dad were with me so he wouldn't dare. Then he laughed and said if they were away then he'd torch their place. He'd burn it to the ground. So Dad rang the police and went around there.'

'Leaving you with the children.'

'Mum was still with me, and we thought the children were asleep. But then Jamie woke and Mum has a bad back and I had to bring him here. And now I don't know what Steve is doing.' She put her face in her hands and her body heaved in distress. Darcy caught her shoulders and held her.

'If your dad's told the police what's happening, there's nothing Steve can do,' he told her strongly. 'You're not to worry. I'll ring the police sergeant myself—just as soon as we get you to bed.'

'Bed...' She gazed wildly up at him. 'Me? No!'

'Your blood pressure's right up again and I'm not risking another convulsion,' Darcy told her. 'I'll ring your mother and tell her, but you're staying here tonight.'

'I...I won't stay in hospital. I can't. Mum will panic. And she can't cope.'

But Darcy wasn't taking no for an answer and Susie wondered just what Kerry's blood pressure was to make him take such a firm decision. It must be dangerously high.

'Your mother's a sensible woman,' Darcy was saying. 'She won't want you driving back to the farm tonight any more than we do. We'll organise the district nurse to give her a hand in the morning, but I'd imagine by then the police will have called Steve's bluff and your father will be there again to help her.'

She cringed, and Susie winced. The last thing they wanted was to further upset her. 'Hospital. No!' She was practically in tears. 'Lisa will freak out. I've only just convinced her I'm going to live as it is.'

'Then stay with us,' Susie said promptly. 'You're not going home tonight, but we can tell Lisa that you've stayed to help us look after Jamie.' Jamie was almost asleep in her arms, but he nestled closer at that, and gave a weary smile. It seemed OK with him.

It still wasn't OK with Kerry, but she was beginning to be convinced. She looked doubtfully at both of them. 'There's no spare beds.'

'Well, well, well!' The tension suddenly broke as Darcy's attention shifted. 'There's no spare beds... Now, how do you know that, Mrs Madden?'

And, in spite of the evening's trauma, a little colour crept back into Kerry's cheeks and the trace of a smile appeared. 'Uh-oh!'

'You wouldn't have had anything to do with the transformation of this house?'

'Who, me?' Her innocent act didn't fool anyone, and Darcy chuckled. It was as much as Susie could do not to stare. Fifteen minutes ago he'd been furious, and now he was responding with…laughter?

'OK.' The gleam was still in his eyes as he went on to part two of his plan. 'We agree you're staying here, and because of you and your accomplices…'

'Accomplices?'

'Accomplices,' he said definitely. 'Partners in crime. If you're partly responsible for a confetti-laden, heart-covered bed, then you get to sleep in it.'

Both women were goggling now.

'You've already got your pyjamas on,' he said. And Kerry had—she'd simply run out the door with Jamie and not thought about what she was wearing. Darcy flashed a quick glance at Susie and then looked away again. She looked stunning—still in her gorgeous bridal attire, crouched with Jamie nestled against her breast. His mouth twisted, but somehow he made himself continue.

'My…my wife is nine months pregnant,' he told Kerry— as if she didn't know. 'She's exhausted, and the bed's totally wasted on us tonight. Therefore I'll sleep in the living room on the settee which you've so kindly left us, and you and Susie will sleep together in your beautifully prepared wedding bed.'

'I couldn't.'

'You could.' He flashed a warning glance at Susie but Susie was there before him, and he could tell she knew what the advantages of his plan were. Kerry had been badly frightened and was exhausted. Her blood pressure was up past safety point, and she needed to be monitored. OK, she wouldn't go to hospital, so let her sleep beside Susie. That way Susie could monitor her beautifully. If she started fitting, her rigid convulsions would wake Susie at once.

It made sense.

'The locals would kill me,' Kerry said doubtfully. 'After all this trouble...'

After all this trouble, Susie's plans for Darcy would have to be put on hold, the bride thought sadly. Her husband's logic was unarguable.

'After all this trouble you're not going to cause us more,' Susie said sternly. 'No one has to know where you sleep. We'll give you a sedative to settle you, and then you'll sleep where you're told. That's an order. And as for us...'

'You don't want me.'

Susie peeped a look at Darcy and she managed a twinkle. Regardless of his anger, she still had plans.

'There'll be all the time in the world for Darcy and I to play in our big new bed,' Susie said. She kissed the top of Jamie's head and held him tight—and then carefully avoided looking at Darcy as her voice firmed.

'After all, we intend to stay married for a very long time.'

CHAPTER NINE

DARCY gave Kerry a sedative. She telephoned her mother who was relieved to hear she was staying put. She listened as Darcy contacted the police, and was reassured that Steve had been located. He was now sleeping off his blustering threats and drunkenness in a police cell. Only then did she allow exhaustion to hit her.

Susie barely had time to give her a thorough medical check before she slept. At six weeks post-Caesarean she shouldn't have been lifting anything heavier than a newborn, but she'd carried Jamie regardless. Thankfully she seemed to have suffered no long-term damage. As Susie gave a relieved sigh, regardless of satin sheets, crimson hearts and confetti, Kerry slept.

Thank heaven, Susie thought, looking ruefully down at her friend. She shouldn't have let her do this wedding organisation.

But then she thought of Kerry's beaming face at the wedding, and she remembered Jamie's enjoyment. It had been a risk worth taking. Both of them had gained from today, even if it had ended in drama.

Kerry seemed fine—but what about Jamie?

She couldn't sleep until she knew he was settled. Leaving her friend soundly sleeping in the bridal bed, she made her way back through the house. Jamie was nestled in his bed, with Darcy sitting beside him.

One glance told her things were OK. Jamie's breathing was back to normal. His colour had returned to a healthy pink and he was speaking seriously to his uncle. Darcy was still in his dinner suit, minus jacket and tie. He looked...

It didn't matter how he looked, Susie told herself hastily.

The things she intended for Darcy would have to wait. Concentrate on Jamie.

'I've spoiled your wedding,' he was saying, and Susie's heart wrenched at the thought.

'How could you have done that?' She stooped to give him a kiss, somehow managing to avoid touching the man beside him. 'We had a lovely wedding. The best. Didn't you enjoy it?'

'Yes, but...'

'But what?'

'But I got sick again and interrupted you.'

'That was after our wedding.' She grinned. 'Your little drama didn't stop us being legally married. The whole thing went without a hitch. Didn't it, Darcy?'

'Yes. Of course.' But Darcy wasn't looking at her. He was concentrating only on Jamie.

Jamie thought about this and decided Susie's words had merit. OK, he hadn't spoiled their wedding, but... 'I've spoiled your honeymoon, then,' he said sadly. 'By getting sick.'

'You spoiled nothing.' Susie wasn't having a bar of this self-chastisement. It was the last thing Jamie needed. 'Your uncle and I were just standing around in our wedding clothes wondering what to do next. I think we felt silly as bride and groom. We make much better doctors. Isn't that right, Darcy?'

'I...' He sounded confused.

He *was* confused. She was too close. Her gorgeous dress was brushing his arm and she was...

'Of course it's right,' she swept on. 'We can't keep on being a bride and groom for ever. So you saved us from a quandary.' She looked contemplatively down at uncle and nephew as Darcy's arms held Jamie tight. The sight made her feel warm all over—but how much did she long to be a part of it?

Concentrate on Jamie...

'You turned us back into doctors simply by showing us an interesting symptom,' she told him. 'Hyperventilation is a very interesting medical phenomenon, and Darcy and I were very interested indeed.'

'Were you really?' Jamie looked confused at that, but a little bit hopeful, and Susie's smile broadened.

'I've never cured hyperventilation with a paper bag before,' she said thoughtfully. 'My textbooks told me how to do it but you're the first patient I've ever practised on. So, you see, I've had a very interesting medical time—as well as a very interesting wedding. All in all, it's been a most satisfactory day.'

Jamie gave this his serious attention. 'I guess saving me was more interesting than being in bed,' he conceded finally, and at last Darcy relaxed enough to chuckle.

'Yes, indeed,' he told him. 'But that's not saying you were at the point of death or that you should try it again. Our Dr Ellis has had her learning experience. She's turned back into a doctor, we're back to normal, so now can we all, please, go to sleep?'

'She still looks like a bride,' Jamie muttered, and Darcy somehow kept his smile straight.

'She does a good job of camouflage. She might look like a bride but underneath the lace she's all white coat, starch and penicillin. And bossy!'

'Really?' The little boy was smiling and Susie relaxed. Great.

'Really,' she said. 'You have no idea how bossy I can get when I don't get my own way. So co-operate now, or I'll have to do something really, really drastic.' She fought for a threat of sufficient magnitude. 'Like...taking the racing wheels off your wheelchair.'

He gave that the attention it deserved, and he grinned, but there was another worry behind his weary eyes. 'I don't have to go back to Kerry's,' he asked anxiously. 'I mean, it was nice there, and when Lisa said I should let you have a honeymoon I thought it'd be great. I thought I wanted to but it was…'

'It was too soon.' Susie nodded. 'You're absolutely right. Your uncle and I both thought so, but you and Kerry and Lisa were so excited we let it be. You'll find we're much sterner from now on.'

'Really?'

'Really.' She cast a doubtful look at Darcy, but then forced her voice to be firm. 'From now on, this is your home. This is where you belong. With me and with Darcy.'

'Because you're my mother and my father now,' Jamie said in sleepy satisfaction. 'And there's me and there's Grandma. There's four of us.'

'And a new baby any time now,' Darcy said, and only Susie heard the note of strain in his voice. 'A proper family…'

'That's what we need to be.'

With Jamie safely asleep, they'd made their way to the kitchen. Susie filled the kettle. OK, she was exhausted, but there were things to be said. Things to be sorted…

'What?' Darcy sounded abstracted, like he intended heading for bed and leaving her behind.

'A family.'

'I know that.'

'So you're going to have to stop flinching every time we're referred to as a family.'

'I don't flinch.'

'You do flinch,' she said soundly. 'Watch.' And before he knew what she was about, she leaned over the table and kissed him lightly on the lips.

He flinched.

She stood back and her eyes narrowed in thought. 'Married couples don't do that,' she said, trying hard to keep it light. 'They kiss back.'

His face shuttered down. 'In case you'd forgotten, this is a marriage of convenience.'

'Not in the town's eyes. Not even in Jamie's eyes now.' She frowned, then turned to pour cups of tea. She didn't need tea, but it gave her something to look at that wasn't Darcy.

The man she loved...

'Jamie needs security if he's to get well,' she told him, trying hard to keep the note of strain from her voice. 'You already know that. He should be on his feet by now, but he won't try. He's clinging to his wheelchair like a security blanket. He collapsed tonight because he wasn't secure. Darcy, he's desperate for a family. For the whole bit. For a mother and a father who love him. And who love each other.'

'I don't—'

'You don't love me?' She turned then and faced him, placing her hands quietly behind her back. Her face was white with fatigue but this needed to be said, and there was no other time to say it. 'I know you don't love me, Darcy, but you're going to have to show affection or this whole damned house of cards will come tumbling down.' She took a deep breath. 'I'm not that bad—am I?'

'No!' He took a deep breath and searched her face. 'You're saying that you can do this?'

'Do what?'

'Love me.'

There. The words were out in the open, like an open wound just waiting to cause pain. And they would, one way or another. Because the time for prevarication was past. Susie was in this with everything she had.

With her whole heart.

'I guess I do,' she said, and the world held its breath.

'You *love* me?' He sounded incredulous.

This wasn't a great start!

'It must be something I inherited from my parents,' she said, trying hard to keep her voice light. 'An ability to love. I seem to do it all the time. I loved my mum and dad, I loved

Charlie, I love Jamie to bits, I love Robert, and I've been watching you for these last few weeks and—'

'You can't!' It was said with such revulsion that Susie backed a step.

'Why can't I?' She pondered. 'I think it's like the chickenpox,' she said at last. 'You catch it and then you're stuck. Like it or not.'

'I don't want it.'

'No?'

'No. Chickenpox only lasts a couple of weeks—thank God—and I never asked for any sort of commitment.'

'I know that.' She somehow made her face expressionless. 'You didn't. But I can't help what I feel, Darcy, and I thought you ought to know what you're stuck with. For more than two weeks. Like it or not, you have that commitment and it's up to you to do with it as you will. I'll ask for nothing from you. But I'm telling you, any time you change your mind and decide you want me as a proper wife—as *your* wife— I'm ready and waiting.'

'Susie, this is ridiculous.'

'It is, isn't it?' she said, and she couldn't quite keep the note of bitterness from entering her voice. 'Like getting married and going to sleep on the settee. Alone. But needs must and I accept it. For tonight.'

'For ever.'

'For however long it takes.' She filled the teacups and handed him one. 'Now, drink your tea and then get on with what has to be done.'

'What has to be done?' he asked warily.

'You were going to check this morning's car-crash victims and make sure that Ian has gone home,' she reminded him gently. 'You were going to turn into a doctor again.'

'Oh, yes.'

'It's easier being a doctor than a husband,' she said thoughtfully. 'But I guess you'll grow accustomed to your new role. In time.'

*   *   *

The teenagers were fine. Ian had allowed two of them to go home, and the other two were sleeping soundly. The boy with the punctured lung was the worst injured but his breathing was deep and even, and there seemed no problem. Darcy was leaning over his bed with his stethoscope when he heard halting footsteps behind him. He turned to find Robert watching him from the doorway.

'He's all right. Pulse is steady, breathing's sound. Ian's had him specialled but I've just reduced the checks to fifteen minutes. They've been damned lucky.'

'They have.' Darcy turned around to face the elderly doctor. 'I thought Ian was looking after things until I took over.'

'Which left Stony Point without a doctor tonight. No. As soon as the bride and groom left, I cut along here and sent him home.' Relieved of his huge workload, Robert was growing more and more responsible by the minute. Any time now he'd be kicking Darcy out and taking over the reins again. Darcy smiled and Robert saw it.

'What's so funny?'

'I was just thinking how much your health has improved. You hardly need two more doctors.'

'Which is just as well if Susie's ready to drop her bundle.' The old doctor rubbed his hands as if he could hardly wait. 'Now that's one confinement you will wake me up for.'

'You need your sleep.'

'Nonsense. These damned exercises and new pills Susie's bossing me into have done me the world of good.'

'Which explains why you're here?'

'With three doctors we don't need an out-of-town medico. I'm keeping an eye on the place tonight.'

'There's no need.'

'Of course there's a need,' Robert was grinning. 'You go on back to that wonderful bed of yours.'

So Robert, too, had been in on the plans. Darcy's face darkened.

The older man was looking at him as if he were an interesting specimen. 'Didn't you like your surprise?'

'Susie did. She thought it was funny.'

'And you?' Robert's face was still thoughtful. 'You don't approve?'

'It's a marriage of convenience,' Darcy burst out. 'How the hell—?'

'How the hell are you going to tell her you don't want her?' The older man pursed his lips. 'I can see that must be hard. When *she* wants *you*.'

That statement took Darcy's breath away. He stepped out into the corridor without a word, and Robert followed.

'You knew!' Darcy said at last.

'Knew what?'

'That Susie's imagining she's in love with me.'

'I'd be a fool not to. It's as plain as the nose on your face.'

'No.'

'Yes. That's why you had no trouble with Immigration. Smelling of roses, the pair of you.'

'Robert, I'm not—'

'Darcy, you are,' Robert said gently before he could finish. 'Of course you are. You're just too damned scared to admit it.'

The whole town was conniving against him.

Robert went home at last, which gave Darcy the run of the hospital. He was tired, but he didn't feel like sleeping. He made his way to the children's ward. Harry was there, still suffering from his bike escapade. His mother had brought him to the wedding ceremony in a borrowed wheelchair, but he'd come straight back in afterwards. The wounds were extensive, he lived on a farm that was none too clean and no one wanted to risk infection.

Darcy expected Harry to be asleep, but the little boy's eyes opened as his doctor entered and he managed a smile.

'It was a cool wedding, Dr Hayden.'

Cool... As a compliment from a ten-year-old, it couldn't be beaten, and Darcy smiled in return. 'Thanks, Harry.' He crossed to the bed and lifted the child's wrist, feeling his pulse. It was a bit too fast for his liking. 'Are you hurting?'

'Just a little bit,' Harry admitted. 'The nurse gave me some pills but...'

'But maybe after the events of this afternoon you need something stronger. If you can cope with a pinprick of a needle, I'll give you something that'll help you sleep.'

'That'd be good.'

He was a brave kid, Darcy thought as he called the nurse and prepared the injection. Maybe too brave. Catapulting down gravel bluffs on none-too-steady bicycles was taking things too far.

Funny... That was exactly how he was feeling, Darcy thought. Like things were careering around him and he was way out of control.

Medicine! Concentrate on medicine!

Three minutes later the injection had been given. Harry didn't whimper as Darcy gave him a mild dose of morphine, and he snuggled down without complaint.

'It'll work in minutes,' Darcy told him, ruffling his hair. 'And tomorrow you'll feel better. By Monday I expect you'll be able to go home.'

'Yeah.'

'Do you want the nurse to stay until you go to sleep?'

'I'd rather you did,' the little boy said pointedly.

Darcy considered it and thought, Why not? After all, all he had to go home to was a settee. So he dismissed the nurse, hauled up a chair and proceeded to wait him out.

He didn't need to wait long. Harry was exhausted and as the drug took effect his eyes fluttered closed.

'Thanks for staying,' he whispered as he drifted into sleep. 'And, Dr Hayden?'

'Mmm?'

'My mum says, preggers or not, our Dr Susie was the prettiest bride she's ever seen. And I think so, too.'

Muriel agreed.

With Harry safely asleep, Darcy tried to think of something else he could do to put off trying to sleep. Check the nursing home, he told himself. In case Robert or Ian had left anything undone.

The only one awake was Muriel and she greeted him with pleasure.

'It was just the loveliest wedding,' she told him. 'Gorgeous!'

'Just because it gave you what you so desperately want...' But he smiled as he said it, and Muriel smiled back.

'If I thought you were doing it just for Jamie and me then I'd feel dreadful,' she told him. 'But she really is lovely.'

'Yes, she is.'

'And it'll be no problem pretending to the authorities that you're marrying for love,' she said sleepily. 'Any fool can see that it's just around the corner.'

'That's ridiculous.' Or was it? 'Anyway, I'm not here to discuss my love life.' Trying to distract himself, he checked Muriel's chart. Her obs were beautifully normal.

'As you'd expect,' Muriel told him. 'You think I intend dying now?'

'I suspect not.' He managed a grin. She'd live for ever, he thought, and as long as Muriel lived Jamie would want to be here.

What had he let himself in for? Indefinite marriage?

'There's no way I'm off to meet my maker now,' she was saying. 'Not when everything's so beautifully settled. Tomorrow they're moving me into a room in the hostel section—around the back, overlooking the creek. Jamie'll be able to run along the verandah and visit me any time he wants.'

But then the satisfied look faded and she frowned. 'That

is, he'll be able to do that when he can run. He will run again, won't he, Darcy?'

'He will.' Darcy touched her wrinkled hand in a gesture of reassurance, pushing his own uncertainties aside in the need to reassure her. 'He hasn't thrown a temperature for weeks. His liver transaminase levels are almost back to normal. From now on it's just a matter of convincing him that the world can be trusted.'

'It can at that.' Muriel sighed happily and lay back on her pillows, content. 'If you knew the weight you've taken off my shoulders… Giving him a mum and a dad.'

'We never—'

But her fantasy wasn't to be interrupted. 'You are, you know. Any minute now he's going to want to call you that, if he hasn't already. And Susie will agree. She's the loveliest lass. You think that, don't you, boy?' Her hand grasped his and there was a trace of anxiety surfacing again. 'I'm not imagining it. You're nutty on her.'

And she was another who knew the truth. 'Muriel, you know this wedding is a matter of convenience.'

'But you think she's lovely?'

There was nothing to say to that but the honest answer. Darcy replaced Muriel's chart on the end of the bed, and he sighed.

'Yes, Muriel. I think she's lovely.'

'Excellent,' Muriel said contentedly. 'My family…'

And how was he to find sleep after that?

'There's dogs everywhere!'

Darcy opened his eyes. Jamie was beside him in his wheelchair and a glance at his watch told him it was ten o'clock. He practically yelped.

'There's three dogs,' Jamie announced.

This wasn't making sense. Darcy threw back the covers from his roughly made settee and concentrated on his nephew. It must have been almost dawn before he'd finally slept and, of course, the alarm was in his…in Susie's bedroom.

'*What* did you say?'

'I said there's dogs in the kitchen,' Jamie said patiently. He had the air of a child supremely in charge of his world. 'Three puppies, actually. There's one for you, there's one for me and there's one for Susie. The black one's mine and I'm calling him Buck.'

'Jamie!'

But Jamie was gone, spinning his wheelchair and heading for the kitchen. 'Come and see,' he shouted. 'Three puppies. Just for us.'

Darcy showered and dressed in record time. Still feeling like he was half-asleep, he emerged to find that there were indeed three puppies in the kitchen.

And so was his new bride, her friend Kerry and his nephew. The three of them were crouched on the kitchen floor and puppies were crawling everywhere. They were about two months old—three fat Labrador puppies—two golden and one black.

They were all very, very cute.

'Where,' Darcy said carefully, stopping in the doorway to avoid standing on a pup, 'did these all come from?'

Susie looked up. She was casually dressed again, in her maternity jeans and enormous windcheater, but she still looked just as gorgeous as she had yesterday. Her hair was tousled, she had no make-up on but she made his heart jolt within his chest. It was crazy, but it felt almost as if his heart hadn't really been operating without her.

'There's been a bit of a mix-up,' she said. Her green eyes twinkled and she picked up the closest puppy and hugged it. 'Now, all we have to do is to decide which one goes back.'

'Which *one*?' Darcy stared. 'Wherever they come from, they can *all* go back.'

'We can't do that,' Susie explained. 'No, Dopey, don't

step in your milk. It's for drinking. You'll offend the towns-folk. Hold him, Kerry.'

'What have the townsfolk got to do with it?'

'It's part of the honeymoon package,' Susie explained, re-fusing to let him get more than a word in edgeways. 'Every-one knows I love dogs, and the postmistress's Labrador had pups just as I arrived back in town. It seems she put one aside for me first thing. As a gift.'

'And then I did the same,' Kerry confessed. She smiled shyly at Darcy, almost as if she expected to be kicked. What had Steve done to her? 'I sort of rang her and said I'd like to give a puppy to you and Susie as my own personal wed-ding present.' She lifted Dopey and cradled him, milky paws and all. 'He makes a gorgeous gift, don't you think? Though I couldn't imagine how to wrap him.'

'And then there was me,' Susie said, flashing a twinkling smile up at her brand-new husband. 'I sort of thought I'd like to give one to Jamie. So I rang and told Mrs Roebottom to keep one, and I told her today'd be a good day to give it to him.'

'And she never said.' Kerry was laughing openly now. 'She took Susie's and my money without a blink and half an hour ago she turned up with three puppies.' She chortled. 'So you have one each. This place will be almost as chaotic as mine.'

'We're *not* keeping them.'

'Which one will you give back?' Susie was hugging one puppy, Jamie was trying to cling to another and Kerry was holding Dopey and gazing up at him with eyes that were far too anxious. 'Maybe we can't. Three people—three puppies,' Susie said happily as she saw the trace of uncertainty in his eyes and knew she'd won. 'We'll be able to walk them to-gether.'

'Susie, Labradors live for fifteen years.'

'Maybe longer.' She tilted her chin and met his look head on. She knew exactly what he was thinking.

'I don't want a puppy!'

'We're not giving them back.'

'Susie, this is ridiculous.'

'It is, isn't it?' she agreed calmly. 'But Jamie and I have had a family vote. The puppies stay.'

'A family vote?'

'Yes.' She twinkled. 'The family vote is two against one and you're outgunned. Maybe when this baby's born it'll be sensible and level-headed and like cats instead of dogs, but until that time majority rules.' She pushed herself awkwardly to her feet and handed Darcy a pup. 'So meet Dopey. Dopey, meet your daddy. He's your latest responsibility, my love. Get used to it.'

CHAPTER TEN

HE NEVER would.

For the next few days Darcy worked in a haze as he came to terms with the fact that he was finally, irrevocably married.

He couldn't forget it for a moment. Even at work it was always there.

The townsfolk thought this marriage was the best invention since sliced bread and they let him know it at every opportunity. Every patient he saw asked about his wife, asked when their...*their*...baby was due, and asked about Jamie and the puppies. They thought the set-up was perfect.

So did Immigration. Three days after their marriage, an official appeared for a spot check. He arrived at lunchtime. Jamie wheeled to the door and let him in, Darcy was kneeling persuading Dopey to drink—well, Dopey had been deemed his puppy and he wasn't gaining weight like his brother and sister—and Susie was serving up lasagne. She greeted the official with cheerful good humour, served out an extra helping and let the meal go on as planned.

Darcy might have been quiet, but between Susie and Jamie and puppies the meal passed in a riot of laughter and chaos. Eventually the official rose to leave and he shook Darcy by the hand.

'There's no problem with this at all,' he said warmly, looking down at the puppy chewing his shoelace. 'Did you say there were more puppies in the litter?'

'The postmistress has one left,' Jamie told him.

'Then I think I'll collect it on my way home.' The official beamed. 'My daughter's been at me for a dog and I've never seen the need, but looking at you people and how much you're giving…' He sighed. 'I just wish all my immigration checks were as happy as this one.'

'Which means we've done it.' Darcy returned after seeing him out to find Susie hugging Jamie in delight. 'That's the last of our obstacles.'

'So we can be a family for ever.'

'Yes.' But then she looked up at Darcy and knew there was one more obstacle to overcome.

Her husband needed to fall in love…

And he wouldn't.

Every night Darcy made up the bed on the settee and lay in the darkness and swore. He'd been dragged into this whether he liked it or not, and he didn't have the foggiest idea where to go from here.

Let go, an insidious voice whispered in the back of his head. You have all the love you need. Susie and Jamie are forming something you can be part of.

But he couldn't take that final step. The bleakness of his childhood held him back, like a tangible chain stopping him from taking that last step forward.

A small tongue crept out and licked his face and Darcy poked Dopey's nose back under the quilt.

'You're not supposed to be here.' Why had Susie allocated him the runt of the litter? he thought bitterly. Dopey needed extra feeding, extra attention, extra love. He was supposed to be sleeping with his brother and sister, but he cried in the night and each evening after he knew Susie and Jamie slept, Darcy threw back his covers and retrieved the little fellow from his basket.

And gave him what he wanted.

Love?

'Labradors live for fifteen years,' he told the darkness. 'I can't take three Labradors back to Scotland. Maybe I'll just take you.'

Another lick, and then Dopey settled himself to sleep against his chest.

Just take Dopey?

And leave Susie and Jamie and Muriel and Buck and Crater...

Hell!

Susie's baby was overdue.

'You're sure of your dates?'

'Of course I'm sure.' Susie was indignant. 'One thing IVF does is make you sure of your dates. I can name the time I met the test tube, right down to the nearest minute.'

'Then you are overdue.'

'Only four days.' She raised her eyebrows at him. 'Hardly enough for alarm—or induction, Dr Darcy, so don't look at me with drips in your eyes.'

'You wouldn't like to go to Hobart and have the baby?'

'No, I would not.' They were treating a farmer who'd rolled his tractor. He'd had a crash bar fitted so what could have been a major tragedy had ended as one fractured ankle. Susie had anaesthetised while Darcy had set it, but as she rose from her stool she winced and Darcy saw it.

'That wasn't a contraction?'

'That wasn't a contraction.' Her humour was fading with the advancement of her pregnancy. 'I'll tell you when I have a contraction.' She thought about it and decided to admit, doctor or not, that she was as nervous as any first time mother. 'In fact, I suspect I'll tell the whole world when I have my first contraction.' She gave a rueful smile. 'I have an awful feeling that I'll yell.'

'Yelling's permitted. Have you been practising your breathing?'

She sighed. 'Yes, I've been practising my breathing. Sir! As my partner, you should be doing the exercises, too.'

He wasn't amused. 'I know how to breathe, but, Susie, you shouldn't be working.'

'I'm not sick. I can still give an anaesthetic. One fractured ankle wasn't worth asking Ian to come for.'

'No.' It had been simple enough, and yet he was still worried. 'Susie, how about if you just look after the pharmacy from now on?'

'And do no medicine at all?' She shook her head, her blonde curls swinging in the way he loved.

He *liked*, Darcy corrected himself. He liked.

'There's still Jamie to look after,' he told her. 'There's some medicine for you.'

'Jamie's back at school in the afternoons now.'

'But he needs—'

'Medicine? Doctors?' Susie shrugged. 'I don't think so. To tell you the truth, I don't know what he needs.' While she talked she was watching Edward Harrow's chest. The big farmer choked and coughed. She lifted the intubation tube away and his breathing dropped straight into regular rhythm. 'Very nice,' she said approvingly, 'I'll bet he's not even sick. That was the lightest anaesthetic I've tried.'

'You're learning.'

As a compliment it wasn't much, but still she flushed with pleasure. 'I've been reading up,' she admitted. 'But I still don't match the level of surgery you're capable of. Now I've realised how much I need anaesthesia, I wouldn't mind doing a short intensive training session. That is, after that baby's born.' She peeped a smile at him. 'If you can cope with all the babies on your own.'

'What—leave me with your baby?' He was appalled.

'I meant the puppies and Jamie.' She grinned at the look of horror that had washed over his face. 'I won't saddle you with a breast-feeding baby, Dr Hayden.'

'Thank God for that. But, Susie...'

'I know.' Her laughter faded as she checked again on her patient. 'You're still worried about Jamie. Me, too. He's losing muscle mass all the time. It's time he was out of that damned chair. But I can't make him try.'

'Neither of us can.'

Susie nodded. 'I've been on to the paediatrician in Hobart and he says we just have to give him time. But, meanwhile, every day he's in the chair he's growing weaker. He should be out climbing trees, doing all the things a boy his age is capable of.'

'He's not capable.' Darcy adjusted the backslab on the farmer's foot, strapping it so the leg was immobile, then watched the process of Edward surfacing to consciousness. He wasn't quite there yet.

'He's not confident.' Susie sighed and put a hand to a back she had to admit was aching. 'That's all he needs. Confidence. And trust.'

'Surely he should trust us?'

'We're not really a family,' Susie said softly, watching her dials instead of her sort-of husband's face. 'Of all the townsfolk, Jamie's the only one who knows our marriage is really a sham.'

'It isn't a sham. It was a legal wedding.'

'You tell that to your nephew, then,' Susie said stoutly. 'He sees how you behave. Say it as if you believe it. And then try saying it to me.'

Damn.

Darcy worked on throughout the day, but Susie's words kept ringing in his ears.

They were ridiculous.

They were blackmail, he thought. She was pressuring him to love her, and he couldn't love on demand.

He couldn't love at all.

But he did love Jamie, he decided. His sister had brought her tiny son home when he'd been a toddler, and Darcy had fallen so hard that when Jamie had needed him he'd dropped everything and come half a world to help.

And, despite himself, he had to concede that if he could have waved a wand and got rid of Dopey the Dog he wouldn't have done it. The puppy seemed to sense that Darcy was his special person and he followed him everywhere.

So, yes, he loved Dopey.

But Susie?

Susie was the limit. The line he wouldn't cross. She was a bossy, organising, matchmaking medico, and she was living with him because he had no choice. That was all.

Why wouldn't she go to Hobart to have this baby?

But why should she? And why was he worrying? There were no complications, Robert had assured him, and she was only four days overdue. But a man couldn't help worrying. After all, she was his wife.

Even if his love extended to Jamie and Dopey, and that was the end of it!

The week stretched on.

Five days overdue.

Six…

The whole town was holding its breath. Everyone was anxious, it seemed, except Susie.

'I'll deliver when I'm good and ready,' she told the other two doctors. 'I have a feeling my baby's much quieter in than out, so if you're looking at induction you can go find someone else to practise on.'

'You're looking tired, Susie,' Robert told her roughly. 'You shouldn't be doing anything.'

'I'm hardly doing anything. One piddly little surgery and anaesthetics when I'm needed. I'm bored. I want to start a young mother clinic.'

'What?'

'I've been reading about them and we had them in England,' she told the men. 'In the cities there are special prenatal clinics for very young mums. We have more than our share of teenage pregnancies at Whale Beach. I reckon I could do something useful.'

'Later,' Darcy told her uneasily. 'For now you go and put your feet up.'

'My feet are fine where they are. My blood pressure's fine, my baby's heartbeat is strong and there's nothing to worry about.'

And there was nothing Darcy could say to change her mind.

Kerry came in to see her that afternoon, still subdued but coming to terms with all that had happened over the past few weeks.

'You're going really well,' Susie told her. 'Apart from the emotional upheaval you must still be going through.' She looked down at her very pregnant stomach and grimaced. 'I'm sorry, Kerry. It must be hard for you to see me like this.'

'No.' Kerry shook her head. 'It's not. I'm not saying I don't ache for my little one but, if anything, you having this baby will make it easier. When I get desperate I can come in here and give it a cuddle and, heaven knows, there are cuddles enough needed at home.'

'The kids are having trouble adjusting to life without Steve?'

'The littlies miss him,' she admitted. 'He was great with them when they were tiny. Playing with them, I mean. He didn't do any of the work but he was fun. It was only as they got older that he didn't like them. But Lisa and Sam are more settled now he's gone. They were both afraid of him.'

'And you?'

'I should have split with him years ago.' She hesitated. 'I...I'm still afraid of him, though. His parents haven't been supportive of him, and he's very angry.'

'He wouldn't dare come near you. The police are watching him.'

'I know. But he's refusing access visits and...well, he's so angry I don't know how it's going to find an outlet.'

'Well, let's just hope he gets into a brawl at the pub,' Susie said roundly. 'Or gets a job where he can vent his spleen on physical work. You have enough to worry about without fretting over him. OK, Kerry, let's check your blood pressure and then you can go check our three puppies.'

Sunday. Still no baby. Darcy was practically climbing the walls.

'Tomorrow I'll induce you.'

'You're not coming near me.'

'I'll get Robert to induce you, then.'

'If Robert says I need to be induced then I agree,' she said serenely. 'Meanwhile, you keep out of it.'

'I wish Robert was here now.'

'For heaven's sake!' It was Sunday afternoon, the hospital was quiet, there were no scheduled clinics and Robert and one of his mates had gone into the bush on a painting expedition. 'He told us where he was, he has his cellphone with him and he'll be back by five o'clock. It's two now. I'm hardly likely to do anything dramatic in three hours.'

'I don't like it.'

'Darcy, if you don't stop clucking I'm going to throw something at you,' Susie said savagely. In truth, this waiting was getting to her, too—plus the fact that she had to be so near to this man all the time and his worry without love was driving her nuts. 'Go and make Jamie practise his walking.'

'You know that's hopeless.'

'Then toilet-train your puppy. He's the worst of the lot of them. Do anything!' She glared. 'Just stop looking at me like I'm an unexploded bomb. Keep away from me, Darcy Hayden, or I might go off!'

'I wish you would.'

'Go!'

* * *

In the end he did have something to do, and it was almost a relief when it happened. The police sergeant rang, looking for him.

'Darcy, we've got a car crash down at Storm Rocks. It's just been rung in. Someone's trapped in the car.'

'Who is it?'

'I don't know. Whoever rang just said they needed assistance because someone was hurt, and hung up before I could get details. There's no farms down that way so I can't find anything out until I get there. But you may well be needed. Will you come?'

Darcy cast an uneasy glance at Susie but she was outside, throwing balls for the puppies. 'Of course I'll come.' Why wouldn't he? 'Fine.'

'See you there, then.'

'Do you want me to come, too?' Susie asked a few minutes later.

'No.' Darcy wasn't happy about leaving his wife, but it was only two hours until Robert was due back. She was showing no signs of labour. 'Val's not here for Jamie, and it sounds like a single vehicle accident. It could be nothing, but it'll take me half an hour to get there and back.'

'Plus the time you're there.' She wrinkled her nose. 'As long as it's nothing serious.'

'I hope it's not.' He stooped and ruffled Jamie's hair and bestowed a pat on his beloved Dopey. 'I have my cellphone, Susie. Ring if you need me. You guys behave yourselves.'

'You should kiss Susie goodbye,' Jamie said thoughtfully, and Darcy grimaced.

He didn't. But, heaven knew, he wanted to.

Five minutes after Darcy left, the phone went again. Susie struggled inside—she struggled everywhere these days—and lifted it, and then frowned as she listened to a voice she didn't recognise.

'Doc...' It sounded muffled and faint, but urgent. 'Is that the doctor?'

'This is Dr Ellis.' She put on her best professional voice and listened intently. She could hardly hear.

'I…I'm having a fight breathing.' The voice stopped as if he was having trouble finding strength to go on. 'Asthma,' he blurted out at last. 'I used the pump but…' The voice trailed off.

'Where are you?' She snapped the command, trying to rouse someone she suspected was drifting toward unconsciousness.

'The Verity farm. I'm looking after it while they're away. I'm… I'm…'

The line went dead.

Hell!

Salbutamol, oxygen, adrenalin…what else did she need for an acute asthma attack?

An assistant, but there wasn't a nurse to spare. She also needed Val to look after Jamie, but she rang Val's home and there was no reply.

Her mind was racing, all the time aware of how quickly asthma could kill. She had to go. The hospital car was available, but what about Jamie?

Should she send him over to the hospital? His grandmother had been taken for a drive for the afternoon by an old friend. He'd hate to sit in the hospital like a patient.

She used to go with her father, she thought, no matter how urgent the call. Why not Jamie?

'Jamie, we have an urgent case out at the Verity farm,' she called. 'Will you come with me in case I need a hand?'

He hesitated for all of two seconds. His eyes lit up like candles.

'You mean a medical emergency? Great. Let's go.'

The Verity farm was about as far into the back of beyond as any farm was likely to be.

'The Veritys have gone overseas to visit their daughter in New York,' Jamie told her importantly as they drove. He was intent on his new role as medical assistant and was racking his brains for information. 'I wonder who's looking after the place. I didn't think anyone was.'

'I don't know who he is, but he sounded sick.'

'With asthma?' He sounded doubtful.

'Asthma can be a pretty frightening illness,' she told him. 'Especially when you're on your own.'

'I guess.' He eyed her sideways. 'Can I really help?'

'Maybe you should stay outside while I find out what's wrong, and then you can come in.' They'd thrown his wheel-chair into the back of the car, but she didn't want him coming in if the man had died. As he well might have, by the sound of him.

He understood. Jamie was one wise child. 'So you want me to stay outside and make myself scarce until you call—in case it's yucky or in case whoever it is hates kids.'

'Got it in one.' She grinned at him. 'You'll make a great medical assistant.'

His small face grew more serious still. 'I hope so.'

Only it wasn't an asthma attack.

Susie knocked on the front door and received no answer. Jamie was pushing his chair out of the car as she knocked. He'd become adept at climbing into the wheelchair himself so she left him to it. Now she gave him a 'stay back' wave, tried the door and found it was unlocked, and went on inside.

The first room was the kitchen. No one. Then the living room. No one there either. Finally the front bedroom. She opened the bedroom door, and Steve Madden grabbed her from behind.

Steve…

She screamed but it was cut off fast and became a muffled gasp as his fingers clapped hard down over her mouth.

'Shut up, bitch, or I'll hurt you.'

'What—?'

But her words were cut off again. A rag was being tied around her face, cutting into her mouth.

'Your fancy doctor of a husband took away my family,' Steve said savagely, and in his voice there was a hatred that was almost implacable. 'Kerry never would have kicked me out if it wasn't for him. She wouldn't have had the guts. So now it's *my* turn to take away *his* family.'

Oh, God, he meant to kill her! Susie struggled wildly in his grasp but she was no match for him. He was big, she was much, much smaller and she was nine months pregnant into the bargain.

'You needn't fight. I'm not planning on killing you just yet. This won't be quick.' He was hauling her wrists together now, and the rope he was using hurt. He was a little bit drunk, she thought, but not drunk enough. 'I'm suffering and so will you,' he told her. 'And so will he when he finds out what happened to you. Eventually…'

He had something planned.

'It'll be nice and slow,' he said, roping her wrists into a knot that cut. 'I've thought it all out. No one comes here. The Veritys aren't due back for months and the chasms in the cliffs are deep enough for my purpose.'

Susie's terrified mind switched from the pain in her wrists and the threats Steve was making. Suddenly all she could think of was Jamie.

Steve didn't know he was here. Please, let him not come in. Please, let him not call out! But Steve didn't know of his presence. Yet.

'We'll take this. I don't want anything to do with you found in the house.' He lifted her doctor's bag, and then paused and opened it. Her cellphone was on top. 'You won't be needing this where you're going. Or your car keys.' He slipped them into his top pocket and he smiled. His smile was pure evil. 'It'd never do if you could call for help—now, would it?'

He pushed her before him out the back door and, blessedly, miraculously, Jamie was nowhere to be seen. Susie stumbled in front of him as he pushed her out behind the house and toward the sea. It was useless to resist. All she'd do was hurt herself—or induce labour. Either way, she had to be passive. For now.

She'd never been so frightened in her life, and ten minutes later, when she saw what was before her, she was doubly so.

Dear God...

The chasm slashed into an outreach of the rocky peninsula, about five hundred yards from the house. To Susie's terrified gaze, it was shaped like a huge grave, maybe twenty feet deep, and it had steep, smooth sides of granite.

For one dreadful minute she thought he intended to push her over the edge, but he looked at her appalled face and he smirked.

'No. You're not getting out of it that easily. I want you to suffer for longer than a couple of seconds while you fall.' He untied the gag from her face. 'I don't want you choking either. That'd be too quick. I want it to be slow. You can yell all you like from down there, and no one will hear you. The sounds of the sea will block everything. You can yell until you die and then your husband will know what it is not to have a family.'

She caught her breath and tried desperately to stay calm. To stay in medical mode. 'Steve, don't do this,' she whispered. 'I know things are bad, but I can help you.'

'Don't call me Steve.' He must be on drugs, Susie thought as she saw the glazing of his eyes and the pinpricks of pupils. His hatred was beyond reason, and she knew he was almost beyond hearing.

They were now at the very edge of the chasm, and she was sick with fear. Beside them was a coil of thick rope which he'd obviously left here some time before. Swiftly, as if he was afraid of being followed, he looped one end of the rope through the knot holding her wrists together. He tested it for strength and then he nodded, satisfied.

'OK,' he snarled. 'Now it's time for you to go where you belong. Sit down and slide over the edge.'

She couldn't. She stared at him in horror but his face was implacable.

'I'll lower you slowly or I'll push you,' he said indifferently. 'If it's any comfort I badly want you alive. For a while. I want whoever finally finds you to know you've suffered for a very long time. So I'll lower you slowly but I can be persuaded otherwise very easily. So get over the side, or I'll push you!'

And, with one final look at his face, she went.

It was the most terrifying thing she'd ever done. Hooked by the wrists, she dangled helplessly, unable to find any sort of foothold in the smooth rock.

Even for Steve it was an effort not to drop her but, mad or not, the man was doggedly intent on fulfilling his plans. Slowly he lowered her, while her arms screamed in agony and her mind screamed that any moment he'd let go.

He didn't. She bumped down, her back thumping in and out against the rocky sides. Finally her feet hit solid rock.

Now what? Susie gazed about her in horror. The chasm was maybe twenty feet long and eight feet wide, and on all sides the rock walls rose smoothly to twenty feet above her. One gap broke the rock wall, and that gap led straight down to the sea, a sheer drop of fifty feet to rocks and crashing waves underneath. And underfoot there was rock and more rock. Not a vestige of vegetation. Nothing.

Her vision of an open grave grew even stronger.

Finally she looked up. Steve was staring down at his prisoner, and his face was twisted into an expression of evil satisfaction.

'I've got a present for you,' he said, and his smile was almost pleasant.

He lifted his end of the rope high into the air—and threw it down on top of her.

'Suffer,' he said. And then, as an afterthought, he tossed down her doctor's bag, which smashed open and scattered its contents over the rocks.

'That's what I think of your medicine,' he said.
And then he walked away.

Jamie.

For the first minutes after Steve left her all she could think of was Jamie.

He'd be by the car. He'd be waiting. Steve had her car keys. He'd go back to the car and move it. Of course, that's what he'd do. And Jamie would be there.

Steve had set this up to hurt Darcy by killing his wife. Blessedly he hadn't included Jamie in his plan, but if Jamie was there she was under no illusion as to what would happen.

She couldn't call out to warn him. To call out to Jamie might let Steve know he was here, and who knew how long the man would stay nearby?

Dear God...

She found a scalpel from her bag and spent a frustrating and painful twenty minutes loosening her wrists. Finally she did it, but it was of no help at all.

God help Jamie...

CHAPTER ELEVEN

'WHERE are they?'

Darcy sounded deeply worried. Robert was back at the hospital, Lorna was with him, Val had come over, and they were all facing a very junior nurse in the hospital foyer.

'All she said was that she was going out to an asthma case and she was taking Jamie.' The young nurse was defensive in the face of Darcy's anxiety. 'She said she'd take her cell-phone with her.'

'It's turned off.'

'She wouldn't have turned it off,' Lorna said. 'She knows the rules about being a country doctor.'

They all did. The golden rule was to stay in contact at all times.

'But my call to a car accident was a false alarm,' Darcy said slowly, thinking it through and not liking it. 'There was no accident. It was a hoax.'

'You think Susie's call was a hoax, too?' Lorna was also looking worried.

'I don't know.' Darcy raked his fingers through his hair. 'Asthma, you said? Wasn't there anything more than that?'

'It was in the middle of visiting hours and everyone wanted me to do flowers.' The young nurse was practically in tears. 'Maybe she said where she was going, but I didn't hear.'

'Great!'

'Maybe there's something wrong with her phone.' Robert was trying to calm things down. 'The battery could well be flat and she's not receiving.'

'It's been too long.'

'Then maybe she took Jamie for a drive after seeing her

patient. If she hasn't figured there's something wrong with her phone then she wouldn't know we'd be worried.' Robert glanced at his watch. 'It's only five. It's hardly time for her to think we'd be worrying.'

'But—'

'It's just because she's so pregnant.' Robert placed a comforting hand on Darcy's shoulder. 'Darcy, calm down. You're acting like every other expectant father.'

'Then why was my call a false alarm?' he said stubbornly. 'Why would someone call the police and report an accident if not to get me out of the way?'

'Now you're being paranoid,' Robert told him. 'Kids make false calls all the time.'

'Sergeant Browning said the caller was an adult male.'

The phone rang in the nurses' station. Lorna left them to answer it.

'Are you sure you can't remember where she said she was going?' Darcy was practically pleading with the young nurse but she shook her head in distress.

'I'm so sorry. I just can't…'

'Look, I'm sure we're worrying about nothing,' Robert said, but then paused as, behind them, Lorna replaced the receiver. He could tell by her face that something was wrong. 'Lorna?' He turned to face her. They all did. 'What is it?'

'I don't—'

'Just say it,' Robert said roughly, and his face was now as tightly worried as Darcy's.

'Oh, Robert!'

'Lorna!'

She caught herself. 'That was the Devonport police,' she managed finally, and she sounded sick. 'There was an accident about an hour ago just outside Devonport. A car ran off the road and hit a tree. According to the identification they found in his wallet, the driver's Steve Madden, but the car he was driving is registered to the hospital.' She took a deep breath. 'They described it and it fits. It's the car Susie was driving.'

'Susie?' The words sounded as if they were dragged from Darcy's lips, and it was almost a groan. 'Was she in the car? And Jamie?'

Lorna closed her eyes, and then somehow found the courage to go on. 'There's no sign of either of them,' she told them. 'They weren't in the car. Steve's unconscious, and by the sound of his injuries it might be quite some time—if ever—before anyone's able to talk to him.'

Susie's back hurt.

It didn't feel bruised. The pain was more than that. She must have wrenched it as Steve lowered her down the cliff face, she thought, because it stabbed like it was on fire.

But she had other things to think about than her back. Like…how was she going to get out of here?

She glanced at her watch for the thousandth time. It was two hours since Steve had dumped her here. She'd explored every inch of her prison and there was no way out.

But overriding every other concern were her thoughts of Jamie.

'Susie?'

The call was so faint that she thought she must be dreaming. She'd been sitting on a rock, but now she jumped to her feet and then winced as the pain in her back struck home again.

'Susie!'

'Jamie!' Blessedly it was Jamie. His worried face was peering over the edge of the cliff, and he sounded as if he couldn't believe it was really her.

'Jamie, don't come closer. You'll fall.'

'I'm lying on my tummy,' he said with injured dignity, and then his voice quavered with relief. 'I thought he'd thrown you over the cliff. I thought you were dead.'

'Well, I'm not…'

'I heard you scream,' he said. 'So I hid, and I hid for ages because I'm scared of Mr Madden, but then after he drove away in our car I came looking for you.'

'In your wheelchair!'

'I found out that I can walk if I hold onto things,' he said, still in that small, scared voice. 'And I crawled a bit. It took me ages to find you.'

'Oh, Jamie...' What he'd been through, to make it this far...

What now? She was fighting to gather her wits—to think of what was best. What they desperately needed was a phone.

'We need to phone for help. Jamie, can you manage to get back to the house and phone?'

'I tried that,' he told her, still slightly affronted that she was doubting his intelligence. 'After Mr Madden drove away I went into the house. The phone's dead. The Veritys must have had it disconnected while they're away.'

Impasse.

Now what? The Verity farm was a good four miles from the main road, and the house was accessed via a rough farm track. Even if Jamie could somehow walk a little, he'd never make it that far. He could use his wheelchair, but if it tipped, or if Steve got rid of the car and came back to gloat...

There was nothing for it. She had to get out of here by herself.

'Jamie, there's a rope down here,' she told him, trying to ignore the messages her back was giving her. She'd been able to do this as a girl, so why not now? 'Steve threw it down on top of me. If I tie an end to a rock and throw it up, do you think you could tie the other end to a tree? Really, really tightly?'

'I'm Cub Scouts,' Jamie said indignantly. 'Course I can. Reef knot or clover hitch?'

'A clover hitch, I reckon,' Susie said, sighing in relief. Bless all Scouts... 'But find a good strong tree.'

'I'm not stupid.' He was still peering anxiously down at

her. 'You think you can climb up the rope? You're pretty fat.'

'Remind me to cross ice cream off my shopping list,' she said dourly. 'Watch your mouth.'

'But you *are* fat.'

'Jamie!'

'And you'll never be able to throw the rope up this high.'

'Stand back and watch me,' Susie said. 'I wasn't Whale Beach junior discus-throwing champion for nothing. Sampson Susie, that's what they called me.'

Sampson Susie did it but it was a Herculean effort. On the third try, the end of the rope landed near where Jamie lay. He took it and spent a good three minutes securing it to a tree. Finally, the rope attached to his satisfaction, he returned to peer anxiously over the edge.

'It's tight enough now for you to climb. If you can.'

But he was right to doubt her. She couldn't climb anywhere.

The back pains she'd been so studiously ignoring were now threatening to overwhelm her. Her rock-throwing had been the last straw. Now she was sitting with her back against a rock and she was concentrating on her breathing like her life depended on it.

'Susie!' Jamie stared down at her, and he sounded terrified.

She couldn't answer him. The pain was overwhelming. How long ago was it since the last wave of pain? A minute? Dear God!

The pain receded then—just a little—and she opened her eyes, just in time to see Jamie slithering down the rope toward her.

'No!' He was her last link with life, and he was trapping himself, too. 'Jamie, no!'

It was too late. He was slithering the last few feet, his wrists twisted into the rope to slow his decent as if he'd done this millions of times before.

And then he was by her side.

*   *   *

'What's he done with them?'

Back at the hospital Darcy was sick with dread. He was pacing as he waited for the police sergeant to arrive, and he was listening to no one. 'He's mad. He's violent and the locals say he's high on drugs. He could have done anything.'

'I'm sure he wouldn't,' Robert said uneasily, though he didn't believe it for one moment.

'Oh, God, where are they?'

'Jamie, you know I'm having my baby?'

'I figured that.' The small boy had crawled over to where she lay. His face was fierce with concentration and worry, and his mind was totally focussed. How could he be only ten years old? 'Tell me what to do.'

He sounded about twenty instead of ten, Susie thought wildly, and she gave an almost hysterical giggle. Then the next contraction rolled in and she found she was gripping Jamie's hand like she was drowning. Ten years old or not, she needed him.

'Just be here for me,' she said.

'I can do that.' He looked down at their linked hands and his wise little face tightened with responsibility. 'I won't leave you alone. But when the baby arrives, tell me what to do, Susie.'

He was a ten-year-old obstetrician but he was all that she had.

'In my bag,' she said between gasps. 'Steve threw it down. There's sterile dressings. Just…just spread them under me so the baby has something clean to be born onto.'

'I can do that.' He started to haul off his windcheater. 'I'll put this under it so it'll be soft.'

'No.' She shook her head, trying desperately to focus on something other than the pain. 'Keep your windcheater on so we have something warm to wrap the baby with.'

He thought that through and found it acceptable. 'OK. Anything else?'

It was a normal birth, Susie thought wildly. A normal presentation. Nothing could go wrong. Unless…

She waited until the next contraction passed and then made herself keep talking. 'Find some scissors, too,' she told him. 'And there's twine. We might need that. Jamie, the only thing that could go wrong is if the baby's born with the cord around its neck. Listen…listen while I tell you what to do.'

Darkness fell over the hospital, but there was no hint of sleep. Every able-bodied person in the district was searching.

But they didn't know what they were looking for.

'He could have put them out of the car anywhere between here and Devonport,' the sergeant said heavily.

Or pushed them over a cliff, Darcy thought. Or buried them. Or…

He was going mad!

'She's nine months pregnant,' Darcy said into the stillness. 'Surely he wouldn't hurt her. Surely…'

It was Susie who was uppermost in Darcy's thoughts, Robert decided as he watched his younger partner. He'd married Susie to protect Jamie, yet now he was crazy with fear for Susie—the wife he hadn't wanted.

So Robert decided he'd just test him.

'I guess this is one way of getting rid of all your responsibilities,' he said softly—and waited for the reaction.

It came. Darcy turned to him with such a look of blazing fury that Robert took an instinctive step back.

'You think I *want* to get rid of Susie?'

'You didn't want to marry her.'

And then Darcy acknowledged to himself what subconsciously he'd known from the moment he'd clapped eyes on her.

'Oh, God, Robert, I love her,' he said bleakly. 'I love Jamie, but Susie's my *wife*. My love. She's my life.'

*   *   *

Nothing and nothing and nothing.

'I'm going out of my mind,' Darcy said. 'Is there no news from Devonport?'

'Steve's deteriorated,' Robert told him. 'They think he's overdosed and that's why he's crashed. They doubt he'll wake.'

'What the *hell* has he done with them?'

Charlotte Louise was born by moonlight. She was born with the cord around her neck, but Susie had explained things clearly. Jamie felt it as the head emerged, and luckily it was loose enough to deal with easily. Without a fuss and with the concentration of someone who knew the world rested entirely on his young shoulders, Jamie slipped the cord carefully, very carefully, over the baby's head. Then he delivered the shoulders and let the little one slide onto his neatly prepared bed of dressings.

After that, the birth was blessedly normal.

Following Susie's whispered instructions—which were difficult to hear when Charlotte was making her presence felt in no uncertain terms—Jamie cut and tied the cord. Then he wrapped the baby carefully in his windcheater and handed her to her mother as though she were the most precious thing in the world.

And as if he was the most experienced obstetrician.

Finally he cleared up as best he could, sat down on hard rock—and burst into tears.

Susie was so exhausted she was almost past speech, but she had to speak now. Jamie had wedged her soft leather doctor's bag under her head as a makeshift pillow. She held her daughter tight in one arm, and with the other she reached out and pulled Jamie to lie beside her.

'Well done, Jamie…'

'We did it,' he quavered, and she hugged him tighter.

'*You* did it,' she told him. 'And now I have two kids. My

two wonderful, wonderful kids. You're the best there is, Jamie.'

His tears dried and he nestled closer. And thought about it. Comforted and safe, the small boy was allowed to emerge from the serious adult who'd just delivered a baby.

'That,' he announced in a voice that barely wobbled, 'was the yuckiest, blurkiest, most disgusting thing I've ever done. Yuck, yuck and double yuck!

'And you did it brilliantly,' Susie said through her own tears, looking at the downy head of her perfect little daughter. 'Oh, Jamie, what would I have done without you?'

'Died?' he said hopefully, and despite all her trauma and her exhaustion Susie managed to chuckle. Jamie's chest was expanding by the minute, and his small-boy ghoulishness was wonderful after the despair of the last few hours.

'I guess maybe I would have,' she told him, because that was what he clearly expected.

He nestled closer, profoundly pleased, but also profoundly weary. It had been some day for a small boy recovering from CFS. 'What'll we do now?' he asked.

She wasn't up to making plans. They'd have to wait. 'I don't know about you,' she whispered, holding him close, 'but, Jamie, I'm afraid I don't have a choice. I'm going to sleep.'

And when Susie woke it was dawn. Jamie was already awake and he had it all organised. He really was the most intelligent child.

'I've been thinking.'

She blinked. 'Yes?'

'Yes.' He was all concentration. 'And I have a plan. There are always firespotters looking over the whole district in the summer. All we need to do is light a fire to attract their attention.'

She thought it through and found a flaw. 'We can't light a fire down here.' It was bare rock.

'So I'll climb up the rope and go back to the house.'

'Jamie, you can't.'

'Yes, I can.' He flexed his muscles—Superman personified. 'See. I'm strong. My arms have been getting stronger and stronger from pushing my wheelchair. And they taught us at Cubs how to go hand over hand so fast you don't fall.' He hesitated and thought some more. 'I'll take my shoes off and throw them up to the top so I can use my toes to help, too. Then I'll put them on again when I reach the top.'

This from a child who'd been wheelchair-bound?

'Jamie—'

'And then I'll find something at the Veritys' farm to light.' He frowned, thinking it through some more. 'It'll have to be something big to attract the firespotters' attention, but I don't think I should set the house on fire. Do you?'

'No,' Susie said faintly. 'I don't.'

'But they won't come if they just think it's a barbecue. It'll have to be something like a shed. Something away from the house.' He brightened. 'Maybe they'll have a woodstack.'

She shouldn't let him do it, Susie thought wildly. He was so young.

But what choice did they have? There was no water down here, and nothing to eat. They were both dry and hungry now, and it was only going to get worse. Soon neither of them would have the strength to climb the rope.

'Jamie, if you're sure you know how to light a fire safely...'

'Of course I'm sure. They've taught us lots of stuff at Cubs.' He grinned. 'I can even rub two sticks together if I have to.'

'Oh, Jamie!'

'But I bet I can find some matches and paper in the house. Now, you're not to worry.' He was sounding more adult every minute. 'It might take me a while to get there, and even longer to light the fire, but I bet I can do it.'

*   *   *

Ten o'clock.

Eleven.

Nothing.

Darcy was going out of his mind.

'Sir?'

Casualty had been turned into a makeshift search headquarters. The boy who entered was in his late teens, and he looked as if he wasn't sure whether he should be there.

'Ben?' The police sergeant looked up as the boy entered. 'What's up?'

Ben fidgeted, still unsure. He was in dirt-stained jeans and a ripped windcheater, and he was almost backing out of the door as he spoke. It was as if he was sure he was wasting their time.

'You know I'm on firespotting duties over the university break?'

'Yes.' The policeman frowned. 'There's no real fire danger today, though. It's mild and there's no wind.'

'No, but I was still up in the tower. It's my job.' He gave a rueful smile. 'I've just been relieved. I know the fire brigade are all involved in the search and the guy who relieved me said we shouldn't worry you with this, but...'

'But what, boy?'

'There's a fire,' he told him. 'It's only a little one, like someone burning a heap of rubbish. It's mostly smoke and it's not moving. It started an hour ago and already it's dying down. Normally we'd send someone out to remind people fire restrictions are in force, but today, with...with all the drama we wouldn't bother. But it's belching a heap of smoke—and it's coming from the Veritys' place.'

'So?' Darcy was so sick with fear that this interruption seemed stupid.

But the police sergeant had focussed.

'You might have something, Ben,' he said slowly. He turned to Darcy. 'The Veritys have been away for months,' he told him. 'Their place is deserted—and it's about the most remote farm in the district. If someone was stuck out there and the phone was out...'

'It is out, sir,' Ben said diffidently. 'I tried it when I came down from the tower, but the operator says the line's been disconnected while they're away. That's what I was wondering. If the Veritys are away, who lit the fire?'

'What are we waiting for?' Darcy was striding out the door before anyone else moved, and the others were left to follow.

The cavalry arrived to find Jamie sitting on the Verity farm gate, waiting for them.

Jamie...

Darcy was out of the leading police car almost before it stopped, gathering his nephew to him in an all-enveloping hug. He shoved his face in the boy's hair and his heart almost stopped, right there and then. 'Jamie, are you OK?'

'Yep.' Jamie was grinning into his uncle's sweater. It had taken longer than expected, but his plan had finally worked. 'I'm not in my wheelchair,' he said proudly.

'I can see that.' The others were out of the cars now—the fire chief, the police sergeant, State Emergency Services officers... Before their eyes, what had been a small wooden outbuilding was a now burnt-out shell. It still poured out black smoke. Jamie had cleared the surroundings, filled the shed with a heap of old tyres and had then set it alight. The residual smoke was black and putrid.

But Darcy only had eyes for Jamie.

'Susie...' he said, and his voice cracked with fear.

But the little boy's grin widened still.

'They're OK, too.'

'They?'

'Susie and our baby,' he told them happily. 'It's a girl. Susie's going to call her Charlie, and I delivered her all by myself!'

Still Susie and Charlotte Louise waited.

Jamie...

Darcy…

They were entwined in her heart, she thought as she dozed and worried and dozed and worried through the long, long morning.

Jamie and Darcy. The two men in her life.

Where was Jamie? She was so frightened for him that she felt sick. Jamie, lighting a fire. Jamie, burnt…

Dear God, she loved him so much. If anything happened to him she couldn't bear it.

It was time for bargaining, she thought. When she and Darcy had married there had been another option they hadn't considered. She was considering it now.

She loved Jamie. She loved Darcy but he didn't love her. Therefore…

Therefore if Jamie was all right then she'd care for him. She'd look after him as her own—and she'd let Darcy go.

'I promise,' she whispered. 'I can cope on my own. I can!'

As if in immediate response to her promise, there was a yell from the top of the cliff and she looked up.

They were both there.

Jamie and Darcy.

Her loves.

CHAPTER TWELVE

DARCY didn't get Susie alone for the rest of the day.

The SES officers reached her first, lowering a stretcher and a team of their men. Then Robert pulled rank and was lowered as well.

'I'm her doctor, and I'm not completely incapacitated,' he growled, so it was Robert who reached her and hugged her first. He reassured her about Jamie and examined her new little daughter.

She gripped his hand and said, 'Darcy.'

He winked and said, 'That husband of yours has been going quietly crazy. It won't hurt to play hard to get for a bit. Let's leave him to sweat.'

She thought that through, but she remembered her promise. She loved him so much, she thought. But she loved Jamie, and Jamie was safe. If Darcy wanted to go...

And then the world moved in. SES men strapped her to the stretcher, and another strapped Charlotte in a cradle against his chest. Then mother and child were carefully inched to the top of the cliff where they were surrounded by joyous well-wishers.

And Darcy.

There was so much he wanted to say, but in the presence of others he could say nothing. He could only watch as she hugged her tiny baby and looked up at him with eyes that were over-bright from exhaustion and relief.

'You look after Jamie,' Robert told him, twinkling at his frustration, and he did. He needed to.

The little boy was covered in scratches and bruises. He was filthy, exhausted and dehydrated, but he was so pleased that he could hardly contain himself. Darcy cleaned him,

178

anointed his scratches, fed him and tucked him into bed. Surrounded by praise and by puppies, the world was his oyster.

'I did it,' he said over and over again. 'I saved them.'

If ever there was a magic psychological cure for a recovering CFS patient, this was it, Darcy thought wonderingly as he tucked his nephew safely under the covers and restrained a pup from licking his face. Jamie had been an unwanted child for so long, and now he was loved and he was secure and he'd earned his place firmly in the ranks of the town's heroes. Darcy looked at the wheelchair sitting beside Jamie's bed, and thought they might just as well throw it away right now.

'I walked,' Jamie said, following Darcy's train of sight. 'I had to. My legs felt really, really wobbly but I walked.'

'You did.' Darcy gathered him to him and hugged him hard. And then he said what had to be said.

'Jamie, you know when I came here one of the kids taunted you and said you should be grateful. That if I hadn't come you'd be a foster-kid?'

Jamie's tired eyes took in his uncle's face. 'Yeah.' He remembered. Kids had the capacity to be cruel, and Lorna had overheard this taunt and passed it on to Darcy. 'I suppose... I suppose he was right,' he said doubtfully.

'No. He wasn't right,' Darcy said strongly. 'It's me who's the lucky one. Not you. If I hadn't come here, I'd never have met Susie. I'd never have had a great kid like you and I'd never have had you around to save my whole family.'

'Your whole family?'

'Susie and Charlotte Louise and you. My whole wonderful family.'

Jamie was tired but he was still game. 'But you don't love Susie.'

'Whoever told you that?'

'You did,' Jamie retorted. 'It's just a marriage so you get to stay here.'

'Maybe it was at the start,' Darcy admitted. 'Maybe it was when I was stupid. But no longer. Now it's a marriage because I love you all very, very much.' He looked down at the squirming puppies and he grinned. 'Even Crater and Buck and Dopey.'

'Have you told Susie that?'

'No,' he admitted, laying Jamie back down on the pillows and watching his eyelids sink toward sleep. 'But as soon as I can tear Lorna and Robert away from her, I intend to do just that.'

Midnight.

She should be asleep, Darcy thought. She probably was. But Lorna and Robert had finally left, the wards were silent and there was no one about. He could just see...

He pushed open the door of the maternity ward and stepped inside, closing the door silently beside him.

Yes, Susie was asleep. The crib was by her side and her daughter snoozed peacefully beside her.

What he had to say could wait. He had all the time in the world, he thought, and there was no way he'd wake her.

He'd pull a chair over to her bed and just watch. For however long it took.

Susie was dreaming and he was there. Darcy.

It was the loveliest dream. There were no rocks, no pain, no threats. Jamie was safe, her little daughter was asleep beside her and the man she loved was by her side.

She opened her eyes, and there he was. Her dream was real.

'Darcy.'

He didn't say a word. For a long, long moment there was silence between them, and then, almost shyly, Susie reached out and took his hand in hers.

'Thank you for coming,' she said, and her voice was absurdly formal.

Hell, where to start?

'Susie—'

'No.' She shook her head and it was enough to stop his initial urge to lean forward and gather her into his arms. He hesitated, and the feel of his hand beneath her fingers sent warmth right through him.

He'd been such a fool. To have this for the taking—and to not take it...

'Love...' It was the faintest of whispers, as if the word was dragged out of him. All the uncertainty in the world was in that word, and Susie misread it.

'I'm not your love.' There was the hint of bleakness in her voice but she steeled herself to keep it back. She'd had such a long time to think things through. All that dreadful morning.

'Darcy, we've been stupid,' she managed.

He'd been stupid. How on earth could she think she'd been anything of the kind? He shook his head. 'Why?'

'Because we don't need to be married.'

How had she figured that one out? The pronouncement took his breath away.

'Why ever not?'

'Because I love Jamie.'

This conversation wasn't going the way he planned. Darcy shook his head again, clearing cobwebs. In truth, he hadn't slept at all the night before, and he was probably more exhausted than she was. Nothing was making sense. 'Susie, I don't understand. I'm sorry.'

'I'm sorry, too,' she said sadly, pulling her hand from his. 'For not seeing it before. But it's the solution to everything. I love Jamie so much. You can't believe how wonderful he was. He can stay here with me. It's as simple as that. I have Robert and Muriel and Val and the whole town to help me care for my two children and my three puppies. We can cope. And you can go back to your beloved Scotland.'

It was as simple as that.

She was granting him his freedom, he thought numbly. He could walk away from all the ties that he'd never wanted.

He could simply walk away.

No!

'But Dopey would pine.' As a gut reaction it was ridiculous, but at least it made her smile.

'You could take him, too. Mind, you'd have to toilet train him to get him on the plane.'

But he was back on track. 'I have a better idea,' he told her, and his voice was so shaky that she could hardly hear him. His hand reached out and gripped hers again. He held her tight, and the terror of the last twenty-four hours came sweeping back. 'If you'll listen.'

'But you—'

'Susie!' It was a curt command and she blinked.

'Yes?'

'Stop organising and shut up for a minute,' he told her.

'But—'

'Or I'll do something drastic,' he warned.

She eyed him sideways, liking the tone of his voice. 'Like what?'

He thought of the direst possible threat, and he just knew that brain needles or enemas or even wheelchair racing wheels didn't cut it here.

'Like kiss you?' he said—and waited.

'Fate worse than death,' she retorted, and then she really heard what he'd said and she gasped. 'You mean, if I don't shut up, I'll get kissed?'

'That's the plan,' he told her.

'But—'

'That's it! You asked for it.' He lifted her into his arms and he did just that.

For a very long time.

And when they finally pulled apart—only inches but enough to get their breath back—things had changed. The world had changed. Susie's eyes were glowing with a million stars. She was lying back on her pillows, her gorgeous curls were splayed out over the white linen and Darcy was looking down at her with all the love in the world, right there in his eyes.

He hardly had to say what was in his heart—but he did all the same.

'I love you, Susie Ellis Hayden,' he told her, and the world righted on its axis—exactly as it was meant to be.

'You…you're just saying that because you've had a shock.' She was still intent on letting him off the hook if he wanted, but he was hooked tight, and it was the most desirable hook he'd ever felt. This woman was his wife. His beloved Susie.

'We had to have an emergency wedding,' he told her.

'Yes, and—'

'And then I stuffed it up by imagining it could only be a marriage of convenience. But, Susie, losing you…'

'Hush.' She put a finger on his lips to stop the tremor. 'I'm safe. We're all safe.'

'We're safe, but I don't want a marriage of convenience,' he told her. 'I want a real one. Starting right now.'

There was joy bubbling within her—a joy so great she thought she'd burst with happiness.

'You mean…me and you? For ever?'

'And Jamie and Charlie Louise and Dopey and Buck and Crater,' he said, and he peeped down at his infant daughter and liked what he saw. 'She's beautiful,' he said in satisfaction. 'Just like her mother. You produce the most gorgeous babies, my love. How do you feel about having another? Not right away, but in a year or two. When we've house-trained this lot.'

'You can't mean it,' she said, but she knew he did. How could she doubt it? This was her happy-ever-after, and it was happening right now. 'You can't really want us. Not for ever.'

'Certainly for ever,' Darcy said sternly, turning back to take her into his arms. 'Certainly for ever, my love. From this moment on, consider yourself properly married.'

'But—'

'No buts.' There was no room for them anyway. No doubts. No buts. Nothing. 'We might have had an emergency wedding, my beautiful Susie, but it was no marriage. From now on, though…this is an emergency marriage. Starting right now!'

Modern Romance™
...seduction and
passion guaranteed

Tender Romance™
...love affairs that
last a lifetime

Sensual Romance™
...sassy, sexy and
seductive

Blaze
...sultry days and
steamy nights

Medical Romance™
...medical drama on
the pulse

Historical Romance™
...rich, vivid and
passionate

29 new titles every month.

*With all kinds of Romance for
every kind of mood...*

MILLS & BOON®

Makes any time special™

MAT4

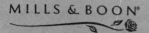

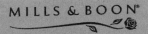

MILLS & BOON®

Medical Romance™

A CHRISTMAS TO REMEMBER *by Margaret Barker*

Part 3 of Highdale Practice series

Dr Nicky Devlin sees Jason Carmichael's desire for her as the perfect chance to repay him for the pain that he has caused her friend. In the run-up to Christmas she realises she loves Jason and the accusations against him turn out to be lies. How can she convince him that her feelings are real after all?

THE DOCTOR'S DILEMMA *by Lucy Clark*

Part 3 of The McElroys trilogy

Falling in love is definitely not on the agenda for ambitious bachelor Dr Joel McElroy. But living and working with the warm-hearted Kirsten Doyle reveals to Joel that she needs some TLC herself. With the arrival of Kirsten's orphaned niece, Joel finds himself drawing closer to this ready-made family—and facing a dilemma...

THE BABY ISSUE *by Jennifer Taylor*

Part 2 of A Cheshire Practice series

Practice Nurse Anna Clemence has tried to keep her pregnancy from gorgeous Dr Ben Cole, but in his desire to get closer to her, he discovers a closely guarded secret. Now he has to convince Anna that he can love this baby who is biologically neither his nor hers.

On sale 7th December 2001

Available at most branches of WH Smith, Tesco, Martins, Borders, Eason, Sainsbury's and most good paperback bookshops.

0801/125/MB19

OTHER NOVELS BY

PENNY JORDAN

POWER GAMES

POWER PLAY

CRUEL LEGACY

TO LOVE, HONOUR & BETRAY

THE HIDDEN YEARS

THE PERFECT SINNER

MILLS & BOON®

FREE!

4 Books
and a surprise gift!

We would like to take this opportunity to thank you for reading this Mills & Boon® book by offering you the chance to take FOUR more specially selected titles from the Medical Romance™ series absolutely FREE! We're also making this offer to introduce you to the benefits of the Reader Service™ —

★ FREE home delivery
★ FREE gifts and competitions
★ FREE monthly Newsletter
★ Books available before they're in the shops
★ Exclusive Reader Service discounts

Accepting these FREE books and gift places you under no obligation to buy; you may cancel at any time, even after receiving your free shipment. Simply complete your details below and return the entire page to the address below. **You don't even need a stamp!**

YES! Please send me 4 free Medical Romance books and a surprise gift. I understand that unless you hear from me, I will receive 6 superb new titles every month for just £2.49 each, postage and packing free. I am under no obligation to purchase any books and may cancel my subscription at any time. The free books and gift will be mine to keep in any case.

MIZEB

Ms/Mrs/Miss/Mr ....Initials ....
BLOCK CAPITALS PLEASE

Surname...

Address...

....

....Postcode ....

Send this whole page to:
UK: The Reader Service, FREEPOST CN81, Croydon, CR9 3WZ
EIRE: The Reader Service, PO Box 4546, Kilcock, County Kildare (stamp required)

Offer not valid to current Reader Service subscribers to this series. We reserve the right to refuse an application and applicants must be aged 18 years or over. Only one application per household. Terms and prices subject to change without notice. Offer expires 31st May 2002. As a result of this application, you may receive offers from other carefully selected companies. If you would prefer not to share in this opportunity please write to The Data Manager at the address above.

Mills & Boon® is a registered trademark owned by Harlequin Mills & Boon Limited.
Medical Romance™ is being used as a trademark.